Peace Out

A Peace Series Novella

By Sandra Hurst

Sky Road Publications

ISBN-13: 978-0-9959288-3-1
ISBN-13: 978-0-9959288-2-4

Production Credits
Editing: T. Morgan Editing Services
Cover Design: Double J. Book Graphics
Published by: Sky Road Publications | Calgary, Alberta, Canada

Dedication

To Rebecca, Taija, Laurie, and Ariel, you kept me believing even when I didn't want to.

To S.H. Pratt, without whom Peace would not exist. And to all the wonderful authors involved in the Peace Project, thank you for the support, the laughter, and the words.

Acknowledgements

To my family – always.

To the pioneers of country music.
Your words have touched so many souls,
including mine.

And especially to the late Mr. George Jones
whose song
Tender Years (Single/1961) was the inspiration
for Cyn and Jericho's story.

Chapter 1

Cynthia Redman flicked her dark braid over her shoulder and eyed the crowd milling around the entrance to the Peace Memorial Gardens with more than a shade of cynicism. It looked like half the town had shown up for Brent's funeral. *It must be the McBride half,* she thought, watching the emotions in the crowd flicker from relief to outright celebration. The Harrington half of town was probably in hiding, wondering what would happen now that the "big cheese" had finally gone.

I should have gone down, Cyn thought ruefully, *if for no other reason than to celebrate with Mrs. Webster and the other victims of the Harrington Mafia.*

The Harringtons had ruled Peace, in one incarnation or another, for the last hundred years. One brutal, grasping patriarch passing the reigns of the family to another in an unbroken line of privilege and excess. The latest Harrington, Brent, had died without an acknowledged heir, so maybe this one-horse town could finally break free of the fifties-sitcom politics and start to grow again.

The police inquest had ruled Brent Harrington's death in a fight at the Deer Lodge Prison as involuntary manslaughter and added a few years to the life of the con who caused it. No one had really questioned what happened. Brent had tried to throw his weight around and picked the wrong inmate to push. Outside of Peace, being a Harrington got him nowhere. He was just a convict in a jail full of convicts.

Still, Cyn thought, *it's no more than he deserves for the way he's treated people in this town—especially Mom.* Cyn squinted behind her dark sunglasses, blinded by the combination of resentment and the weak November sunshine. The whole Harrington fiasco infuriated her. She had learned not to ask too many questions about her mom's past in Peace. *But,* she mused, *something bad must have happened between Mom and Brent Harrington.* There had been far too many conversations that died out as soon as she walked into the room, far too many unexplained glares from her mom when the Harrington name was mentioned.

Pulling the collar of her winter jacket up around her ears, Cyn started the trudge back to the clinic. A black Durango flew past her showering her with mud and ice. *David Falton,* she thought resentfully as the blond driver of the truck waved at her in the rear-view mirror. *He's such an ass!*

Shaking her coat to remove the worst of the mud, Cyn rushed along main street and toward the clinic. Mrs. Webster would be there for an appointment at two o'clock, and it would take time to turn on the space heaters and get the room warm before the client arrived. The therapy room would be cold—it always was, there was just no way to keep it warm in there, not in November.

Cyn loved being the receptionist at Redman Holistic Counselling. She was so proud of the way Bev, her mom, had built the practice from the dirt up, back when no one believed that counselling was a real thing. Beverly Redman had raised her daughter in Billings, working for a local law firm and taking courses at night. Eventually, once she finished her social work degree and added it to the mix of holistic practices and lifestyle management that she taught to her clients, she finally came home to Peace and set up shop.

But that happened back when I was in grade nine. Cyn sighed to herself. It was all over now. Cyn screwed her eyes closed against the tears. The wind was making her eyes water again. *Yah,* she thought, determined not to show weakness, *it's the wind.*

This would be the last year her mom took patients at the clinic, and in three weeks, just before Christmas, the cozy storefront centre would close forever. *Hopefully, after the New Year,* she thought, *we'll have new tenants for the space.* The rent they paid would add a bit more breathing room to their meagre budget and start paying off Mom's crushing medical bills.

The realtors had been through two or three times last week, poking in corners and banging on walls. "What do they think," her mom had joked, "that I have a body buried in there?"

Cyn opened the frosted glass doors that led into the clinic, letting the familiar smell of sage-grass and the earth-tone colours of the reception area warm her heart. Hanging her black pea-coat on one of the hooks, she peeked into the therapy room to see if her mom was in yet. Mom hadn't been to the funeral either, the doctors said no, it was still too soon after the surgery.

"Hey, little one." Her mom's voice still sounded a bit thin, but it was filled with the gentle warmth Cyn had always loved. "I'm in the storage room. How was the service?"

"I didn't go, Mama," she admitted. "I'm hardly sorry Brent's gone and going just to celebrate felt wrong." Cyn stomped her feet on the woven rug in front of the door, trying to shake the snow from her boots. "There were a ton of people there, though. I saw enough just standing on the road."

Cyn just couldn't imagine life without the tiny woman who was emerging from the back of the clinic. A figurine—no, a doll—would look stronger, a paper doll.

"Now hush your brain, Cynthia!" the birdlike figure scolded as she shuffled carefully down the corridor from the storage area. "I can hear you worrying from all the way over here." Bev Redman smiled at her daughter, taking the sting from her words. "Just like we decided, no worrying for now. The doctors think we're safe.

We'll wait until the biopsy results come back and see if there is anything to worry about then."

"Right, Mama," Cyn said, shoving her heart back down her throat. "No worrying."

So many times, Cyn had heard clients come into the centre and tell her mom that they felt like they were holding on by their fingernails. Mom would always tell them to embrace their own hearts. To put band-aids on their own wounds, to hug themselves, even when no one else would. Cyn had always thought it was a stupid, trite expression, but she'd kill to believe it now. If the surgery hadn't worked, there wouldn't be any more trite expressions, no more aura readings, no more psychobabble, and possibly, no more Mom.

Her heart died a little every time she saw the frail shadow that cancer had left of her mom, every time they got reminder letters for the medical bills they just couldn't pay, or notices from the University offering her a route to her psych degree that they just couldn't afford.

Yah, she was falling apart. Her heart was wrapped in bailing wire, its razor-sharp threads were all that held her together now.

"Mrs. Webster will be here soon," her mom said, fluttering birdlike hands in the general direction of the therapy room. "Would you mind turning the temperature up a little and putting something calming on the stereo? Her history with Brent will make this a hard day for her. She drove back from her daughter's house in Deer Lodge just to attend the funeral."

"Sure, Mama, right away." Cyn brushed past the slowly moving stick figure and hit the light switch on the therapy room. The furniture was warm and welcoming. Just a big soft sofa with lots of pillows to cry on or even to throw and stomp over if that was what was needed, and Mama's big papasan chair, so out of place with the southwestern décor, but Mama swore that she couldn't work without it.

The cracked, peeling wicker of the chair was rough under her hands as Cyn moved the chair closer to the chipped ceramic floor heater that sat in the corner. Gentle Aztec flute music filled the small room, settling her heart a little as she placed a few extra blankets around the room, just in case Mama got cold.

Mrs. Webster showed up on time and carrying a huge to-go cup of coffee from Generic Eric's, as always. Cyn greeted her with a real smile, the first one of the day. "Did Eric talk you into working this afternoon, Mrs. Webster?" Before retiring as the longest-serving waitress at Generic Eric's, Mrs. Webster had built a tolerance to their high-test coffee that was truly astonishing.

Her grande triple espresso with a shot of hazelnut would take the edge off the cold without giving her even a mild buzz.

"Good morning, Cynthia," Mrs. Webster replied. "Not a chance!" She laughed and waved her cup around, sloshing coffee onto the polished hardwood floors. "Eric knows I'm not moving back to Peace. I only came back to town for the funeral and to do the paperwork for selling my house, then it's back to Deer Lodge. My grandbabies need me." She slid off her jacket. "Cynthia, be a dear, would you?"

Wrinkling her nose at the hated long form of her name, Cyn stepped past the wooden reception desk and took Mrs. Webster's coat. "Certainly," she said. "Doctor Redman is waiting for you in the therapy room."

"Did you go to the funeral this morning?" Mrs. Webster's faded blue eyes twinkled merrily. "I haven't seen so many old friends in one place since Dexie McBride came home and got married, and that's been a few years now!" Not stopping to hear an answer, Mrs. Webster drifted past, her paisley cane leaving muddy pockmarks on the laminated wood flooring. *Great,* Cyn thought, hanging Mrs. Webster's coat on the polished wooden coat-tree and grabbing a rag for the coffee and cane marks. *No worries, Mrs. Webster, I'll clean that up!*

The door of the therapy room swung closed and the two women's voices could be heard exchanging muted pleasantries. Flipping the small switch under the reception desk, Cyn started pulling her coat and shoes back on. A flashing light in the therapy room would let her mom know that she was away from the desk.

The late November wind sent a shiver down her spine as Cyn stepped out of the clinic and carefully locked the door behind her. November hadn't been a good month; the sidewalks were covered in a grey slush made up of half-hearted snow and the mud kicked up by the transport trucks that rattled down main street at all hours, not stopping, all going somewhere more exciting than Peace.

Cyn pulled a wry face as she saw six trucks with McBride Ranch logos parked out in front of Generic Eric's. So much for grabbing lunch there, she thought. If the McBrides have all their men in town, there won't be a seat left.

Complaining to herself, Cyn slumped off the sidewalk and headed across the street toward the grocery store. They usually had soup or something on sale. It was better than an empty stomach on a cold day. She didn't even see the dirty brown pickup truck until it veered away from her and slammed into one of the garbage cans that were cemented to the sidewalk up and down main street. A tall man unfolded himself from the cab, cursing quietly. "Miss? Ya'll okay? I didn't see you there."

Cyn shook her head and kept walking away until a hand grasped her shoulder.

"Are you okay? Answer me, please!" The deep voice with its hint of a southern accent was quiet but firm, and the hand that gently shook her shoulder knocked Cyn out of her daze and somehow centred her thoughts.

"You..." Cyn's voice was shakier than she thought it would be. She swallowed thickly and tried again, "You almost killed me."

"You need to watch it when you step out into the street, ma'am. Peace may be small, but we do have cars here."

"Who are you to talk to me about Peace," Cyn said, her dark eyes flashing. "I've lived in this litterbox since junior high school."

"My name is Jericho Matthews." Jericho let go of his grip on Cyn's shoulder and stepped back slightly, politely ignoring the fact that the shaking hadn't gone away yet. "I work up at the McBride ranch. Don't come into town much, so I guess we haven't met."

Cyn looked up at the cowboy. She couldn't believe just how far *up* she had to look to meet his dark-brown eyes. She tilted her head back so that she could look at his face rather than his chest, nice though it was. Cyn scowled, trying to get a sense of the man from his features. She wished her mom was here—Mom could see through people like they were made of glass. "Let me go, please, Mr. Matthews. I need to get back to work." Cyn tried to keep her voice steady, but it still sounded shaky and much younger than the twenty-six year-old she really was. "I'm sorry that I didn't watch what I was doing. I hope your truck isn't knocked up too bad."

Damn, Cyn thought, *that's all I needed—truck repairs are just one more thing I can't afford to pay for and I will not worry Mom about this kind of stuff.*

"Not to worry, Miss...?" He made the polite statement a question and Cyn sighed ruefully. She hadn't told him her name. She was kind of hoping not to. Cyn had decided months ago that she didn't have room in her mind for anything other than her

10

mom and their future. Everything else, everyone else, was unimportant.

"Redman," she finally admitted, when it looked like Jericho was going to stand there until she gave him a name. "I'm Cynthia Redman. I work at the counselling centre across the road."

Jericho took her hand and held it gently. *His skin looks so dark against mine*, she thought. Cyn had never had her mom's beautiful copper skin.

"Let me walk you back, Miss Redman," Jericho said, giving her a guiding push back down the street toward the clinic. "You still look really pale, and I'd feel better if you were inside somewhere warm." As Jericho steered her down the slushy sidewalk and back toward the doors of the counselling centre, Cyn couldn't help stealing glances. He was an anomaly in a town full of bellowing ranchers and chirping old ladies. He didn't talk much, didn't ask questions, just walked quietly beside her with his hand once more resting on her shoulder.

Cyn climbed the steps to the clinic door and turned back to say thank you, but Jericho had already turned to go, heading back toward his beat-up truck with a lope that made it obvious just how much he had slowed down to walk with her.

"Mr. Matthews!" Cyn called after him. Jericho stopped and glanced over his shoulder in surprise. "Please make sure you let me know how much I owe for the damage to your truck."

"Why,"—he smiled, teeth flashing ivory in his black face—"this old piece of junk isn't worth worrying about, Miss Cynthia," he said. Cyn thought she picked up the occasional hint of a drawl giving away his southern background. "It's already held together by nothing more than bailing wire and good intentions. Just teaches me right for coming to town when I didn't need to."

"Well, I'm glad you did," Cyn said softly, but loud enough, maybe, for him to hear her. "Thank you."

Jericho tipped his worn black Stetson and turned back to lean over and mutter at the grill of his beat-up Ford. Pulling off his weather-beaten duster, he bent to lay it down on the mucky sidewalk. Setting his Stetson on the hood ornament, he knelt on the duster and bent double to get a look under the grill. Fortunately, this gave Cynthia a prime view of an unexpected asset. And man, what an asset. Jericho's firm rear was covered with denim that looked as soft as leather and fit tight in all the right places. *Damn,* she thought, then shook herself mentally, turned away from the tempting sight, and walked inside.

Cyn closed the office door quietly and flipped the switch under the reception desk that would flash again to let her mom know she had returned. She'd forgotten entirely about her lunch, but since she was still a bit shaky from all the excitement, she didn't feel hungry at all.

Picking up the file for the next patient, a Ms. Todd who came by once a week for counselling, Cyn set about doing the accounting for the day only to catch herself a few minutes later staring out the front window of the clinic and wondering if Jericho was still out there, bent over his old truck, showing off his assets. *What the hell am I doing?* Cyn thought. *I don't react to guys like this. He's just another blowhard cowboy! So why am I scared? Why do I feel like meeting this quiet-spoken man has changed me somehow?*

Chapter 2

Valerie Todd showed up early for her three o'clock appointment. Sidestepping quickly, Cyn only just avoided a collision with Mrs. Webster, who was rushing blindly out of the office, face puffy and red from tears. Cyn took Valerie's coat, showed her into the therapy room where her mom was waiting, and closed the door.

For the next few minutes, Cyn sat quietly at the reception desk, working on her overdue assignment for Psych 101 and wondering if she would ever get a scholarship so she could stop taking online courses and actually go to University. She was determined to learn real psychology, the kind you practised in a hospital, not in a back-room filled with crystals and chakra images. She looked enviously at the *University of Montana – Bozeman* stamp on the printout from the distance-learning course. Even before her mom got sick, they hadn't really been able to afford University for Cyn. Hell, they couldn't afford to fix their beat-up Prius.

Cyn was surprised when the door to the therapy room opened at 3:15 p.m. and Valerie came out alone.

"Dr. Redman isn't feeling well," she said, stopping at the front reception to grab her coat and boots. "She asked me to rebook for tomorrow."

"I'm so sorry for the inconvenience." Cyn's response was distracted, automatic. Nothing had ever made her mom cancel a session, not even the cancer treatments. "Can you come tomorrow at two o'clock?"

Ms. Todd smiled, nodded, pulled on her bright-red parka, and with a wave, showed herself out the door.

Immediately, Cyn turned to the therapy room only to find the door shut. The door knob just rattled when she tried to enter. It was locked.

"Mama?"

"I'll be out in a few minutes." Her mother's voice was thick, and Cyn thought she was speaking through tears. "I'm okay, don't worry. Get the day sheets ready for me to sign, please. We have to get them off to the insurance companies before we leave tonight."

The large Kokopelli wall clock in the reception area seemed to vibrate with each tick, every sound grating along Cyn's nerves. Cyn's eyes glanced back and forth from the locked door to the paperwork on her desk as she anxiously waited for her mom to come out.

How long had it been since Ms. Todd left? Half an hour? More? When filling out insurance forms and moving the stacks of paper on her desk from place to place wasn't distracting enough, she started the weekly cleaning routine. Cyn bustled around the reception area madly dusting and organizing, trying to ignore the closed door that loomed at the west end of the room. She needed to keep the routine going. After all, there would still be clinic hours for the next few weeks, patients to see, paperwork to submit, it all had to be done, just as if nothing was happening.

Finally, her mother's voice came from the therapy room. "I'm working on some notes on the session. I won't be much longer." A few minutes later, the door to the therapy room opened, and a pale, red-eyed Bev Redman emerged with a file folder tucked under one arm. Her other arm trailed along the wall as she moved carefully toward the reception desk. *Her balance must be acting up again,* Cyn thought. The medications did that some days. "Are you ready to head home, Mom?" Cyn said, collecting her laptop, keys, and the beat-up black knapsack she hauled everywhere she went. "I put chicken in the slow-cooker this morning, so dinner will be almost done when we get there."

"Sounds good, little one," Bev said. "I'm not sure if I'm hungry, but I'll try."

"Are you okay?" Cyn's dark eyebrows shot up. Her mom never turned down food. Even bad days were never *that* bad.

Bev's smile was distracted, and her dark eyes flashed from Cyn to the unmarked folder she carried. "A bit of a complication on one of the cases I'm dealing with. Don't worry about it, Cyn. It's work, it's not me." Bev made a shooing motion at Cyn. "Go get the car warmed up. I'll be out in a moment."

Cyn stepped out of the small front reception area, but rather than head to the back door where the car waited, she stood silent for a long moment, worrying over her mom's strange behaviour. Resolved, Cyn pressed the car's auto-start so it would warm up, then turned back and quietly peeked into the office to check on her. Through the open door Cyn could see Bev making her careful way to the big bookcase in her private office. Groaning as she pulled a copy of the Montana Code for Mental Health Professionals from the top shelf, Bev wrestled the heavy legal text into her briefcase, almost dropping it several times. Cyn had to restrain herself from helping, but she didn't want her mom to catch her hovering like this, especially after Bev had told her to go. Every health professional was required to keep a copy of the thing, but damn, Cyn didn't remember it looking so heavy when she had last leafed through it. *That was years ago though,* she thought. *Back when Mom took her courses in practice and legal ethics.* With a muttered curse, Bev hauled the loaded briefcase off the floor. Quickly tiptoeing out the way she'd come, Cyn eased the door to the building closed behind her. She got as far as standing next to the Prius before Mom appeared a moment later. Locking the door behind her and grabbing the railing for balance, Bev made her way down the icy stairs.

"What took so long?" Cyn complained, rubbing her cheeks to bring some heat back into them.

"It wasn't that long," Bev retorted. "You didn't have to stand out in the cold waiting for me." Stepping past Cyn's outstretched hand, she clambered into the passenger seat of the beat-up blue car. "I'm not useless, I can come down my own stairs!" The inside of the old Prius was warm and comfortable. Bev turned toward where Cyn was struggling to fasten the seatbelt, her cold fingers making it an awkward job. "You have to stop this, Cyn," she said quietly. "You know the doctors have said I've got a good chance to beat this, but you need to start believing it." Bev's voice dropped to a bare whisper, hardly audible over the hum of the heater fan. "I need you to believe it. I can't hold off my fear and yours as well."

Cyn tried to smile but ended up coughing. "I know, Mama." She said tiredly as she threw the car into gear and headed for home. "Time for dinner?"

Chapter 3

The hellish creature crouching next to Cyn's bed started to howl at 7 a.m. Cursing mornings, alarm clocks, and the cold floor, she dragged herself out of bed and into her jeans. *It's Saturday, at least,* she thought. *No clinic today, just paperwork and studying.*

Staggering into the kitchen, she was surprised to find the coffee pot was already brewing. Her favourite cup sat in front of it, sugar and milk already added. The smiling minion on the front winked its single goggle-eye at her. Cyn checked the clock on the stove. Yep, 7:09 a.m. "Mama, what are you doing up so early on a Saturday?" There was no answer. "Mama?" Still nothing. The silence stretched out, broken only by the last drops from the coffeemaker dripping into the pot. Cyn hurried down the long hallway of the mobile home they lived in and stopped at the half-closed door of her mother's bedroom. The *tap, tap, tap* sound of a keyboard told Cyn where her mom was. Leaning against the wall in the passageway, she closed her eyes. Her shoulders slumped in relief. A small, quiet smile drifted over her face. It had been a long time since her mom had felt well enough to write; it was a good sound. Maybe the medication was going to help after all.

"Are you ready for breakfast, Mama?" she called, being careful to avoid pushing the door further open. Writing time was sacred—that rule had stood since before Cyn did. "I'm going to make some French toast; do you want some?"

"Sure, baby, sounds good." Bev sounded distracted, but her voice was strong and purposeful. "Give me half an hour, this report needs to be finished today."

It took longer than she said, it always did. But finally, Cyn heard the clicking on the computer stop. Grabbing the old cast-iron frying pan, the one that never burned anything, no matter how distracted she got, Cyn started cooking. The warm, sticky smell of cinnamon French toast drifted through the kitchen.

Bev came out of the bedroom and sniffed appreciatively. "That smells so good," she said, dropping a stack of folders on the worn kitchen table. "I'm really hungry today!" A few syrupy moments later, Bev leaned back, licking her lips. "So good, Cyn! Remind me to hire you!" Cyn grinned. It was so good to see her mom enjoying life and relaxing. Every day she seemed a bit stronger, a bit more like the mom Cyn remembered, and less like the wraith that had drifted around the house for the past few months. "I need you to drive me to the State Law Library in Helena." Bev's voice was distracted as she leafed through a particularly thick red folder.

"Helena?" Cyn questioned. "Can't you use the

library here in Peace or the big one in Billings?"

"This is a bit obscure," Bev replied, "and I need specific resources that aren't available here. We can stay overnight and drive back on Sunday."

"What are you researching, Mama?" Cyn asked, picking up the dirty plates and dropping them in the sink with a clatter. She normally tried to keep out of the psychological side of the practice, but it had been ages since she'd seen Bev so involved in a case.

"Cynthia Ann Redman!" Bev's voice was sharp as she glared warningly at Cyn. "Confidentiality! You know I can't talk about cases, even with you."

Cyn recoiled, shoulders snapping back. The reprimand was almost physically painful. "You know I..." Cyn started to run water into the sink, trying to keep her face turned away from where Bev scowled over the empty plates. *It's too much,* she thought, diluting the soapy water with a few bitter tears. *This is the first day in ages that Mama has acted normally, and now it's ruined.*

A gentle touch on her back interrupted Cyn's moping. Dragging the rough flannel of her shirt over her red eyes, gritting her teeth in an attempt to smile, she turned slowly back toward her mom. "That was uncalled for, Cyn, I'm sorry." Her mom's eyes were solemn, the normal twinkle missing from their berry-brown depths. "This case has me worried, but I shouldn't be taking it out on you." Grabbing her big briefcase, Bev wrestled it to the table and started loading the red manila folder into it. "I can't say much about it, of course." She smiled, softening the words this time. "All I can tell you is that I need to make a decision about a client, and it's complicated. I need to look at some legal textbooks."

Quickly finishing up and drying her hands, Cyn grabbed her well-worn coat from behind the door, picked up the heavy briefcase, and gestured toward the trailer door. "Helena is a long ride, Mama," she said. "Should we stop at Eric's for some coffee to-go? We've finished the pot from this morning."

"Coffee sounds wonderful," Bev said. "But not from Eric's, not today."

"That's weird," Cyn said, dark brows furrowed, trying not to appear too curious, "but whatever. We'll stop on the highway, then." Cyn shrugged and grabbed the two huge to-go cups from the counter. "Sonic's coffee isn't that bad."

Four hours and a rest stop later, Cyn pulled up to the Justice Building off Sixth and Sanders in Helena and waved as Bev got out and hauled the big briefcase to the curb with a thud. "Don't sit and wait for me," Bev said. "Go book us into a hotel and get something to eat or do some work for your psych class. Just come by and pick me up when the library closes at four o'clock. If I'm ready before then, I'll text you."

Pulling away from the curb, white-knuckled hands gripping the steering wheel, Cyn moved cautiously into the city traffic. *As much as I'm dying to get out of Peace,* she thought, *I guess I'll always be a country girl. This many people make me jumpy.* At least it was the weekend, when downtown Helena wasn't quite so busy.

Checking herself into the Baymont Inn about a mile from the library, Cyn dropped their small overnight bag in the room, grabbed her phone and her knapsack, and walked into the chilly November sunshine. There had to be a coffee shop close by where she could find some decent coffee and work on her latest assignment.

Slowly making her way down the slush-filled pavement, Cyn shuddered as she walked past the flashing sign for McDonalds—she wasn't that desperate. It wasn't more than a block further down Prospect when her nose twitched, and the rich smell of freshly ground coffee beans drew her toward the bright-green doors of the City Coffee Company. Cyn's stomach grumbled as she looked at the loaded bakery counter at the back of the restaurant. Coffee at the Sonic on the highway had been a long time ago, and breakfast longer than that. Finally deciding on a sticky walnut bun and a bucket-sized hazelnut latte, Cyn settled into one of the brightly lit booths and sighed happily. This is why she wanted to live in the city; wifi access instantly with no the-front-loader-knocked-down-the-repeater nonsense.

Within two minutes she had her laptop connected and was plugging away at her assignment for psychology. She was two weeks behind but had been granted an extension due to her mom's health issues. She needed these credits if she was ever going to get into the actual program in Bozeman. Following her mom into counselling was all Cyn ever wanted to do, but not like mom did it. She wanted to work in a hospital, with people who were genuinely ill, not trying to improve their karma or re-live their past lives. Giving herself a mental shake, Cyn let go of the old argument. Her mom would never outgrow the 70s star-child lifestyle. She would always believe in crystals and tea leaves, but Cyn just couldn't. She'd seen too much, felt too much.

Head down in her laptop, Cyn spent a concentrated hour trying to force her mind through the intricacies of cognitive therapy. *It's overwhelming,* she thought, *there's just so much to know!* It wasn't until she stretched, shoulders protesting and neck sore, that the deep voice at the bakery counter caught her attention.

Cowboy, she identified and rolled her eyes inwardly. *And here I thought Helena would be a break from them.* The sweet aromatic bite of fresh spices had her nose twitching appreciatively. Her coffee was cold, and she really did need a refill. Getting up, she joined the line at the counter and gave the man in front of her a quick appraisal. He was tall and broad-shouldered, wearing a muddy black duster and old leather-soft Levi's. Her breath caught in her throat. It was Jericho Matthews. *Just breathe,* she thought. *Slide quietly back into the booth, unseen and unassailable.* The more instinctive side of her was busy appreciating the breadth of his shoulders and the butter-soft leather of the old duster he was wearing. *Move now,* she tried to tell herself. *You can watch his ass from behind the laptop where no one will know that you checked him out.* Caught between appraisal and retreat, Cyn's moment passed.

Jericho turned away from the cash register, the cup he was holding banging against her arm, its scalding contents pouring out all over the floor and staining the moss-green sweatshirt she had thrown on this morning.

"I'm so sorry, ma'am," he apologized. "Miss Cynthia? Now I'm really sorry!" There was definitely surprise on his face, but Cyn thought she saw a flash of something else as well. *Why on earth would he be embarrassed?* she thought. *It's just an accident.*

Dumping the dregs of his cup into the steel sink on the counter, Jericho shoved the empty cup into the recycling. "Did you get burned, Miss Cynthia?" He asked, frown lines creasing his usually smooth face. Grabbing a paper napkin, he dabbed gently against her reddened forearm.

"I'm fine, Mr. Matthews," Cyn replied with a slight wave. "It was just coffee, don't worry about it."

Cyn felt her heart flutter and slammed the lid hard on her wayward emotions. But she had to admit how nice it felt having someone concerned about her. Someone Cyn didn't need to look after. *Cynthia Ann Redman, get over it!* she scolded herself.

"What brings you to the capital today?" Jericho asked, his voice dark and as soft as fine chocolate. "It's a long way from Peace just to get a coffee."

"My mother had business in the city," Cyn said, "so I drove her into town and sat here to get some studying done."

"Studying on a beautiful day like this?" Cyn was almost blinded by the flash of Jericho's smile. She couldn't remember seeing him smile before. Maybe he didn't smile often, but it was amazing. "It seems a waste."

Cyn surprised herself by giggling. *I am not a giggler,* she thought. *No matter how nice his ass might look in those jeans, this isn't going to happen!* "I was just getting up to grab more coffee when I saw you and...

"And I spilled my drink all over you," Jericho finished her sentence. "Well the least I can do is buy you one. What were you drinking?"

"You don't need to—" Cyn's protest was cut short by a wave of his strong hand.

"Please, let me," he said. Turning to the girl behind the counter, he gestured for Cyn to put in an order.

"Hazelnut latte," she said, wondering if he would laugh at her girly drink. Jericho didn't even blink.

"A large hazelnut latte, please." He said, "And for me..."

The girl behind the counter winked at him saucily, her blue eyes more than a little interested. "A fresh Chai for you, coming up."

"Erm." On a fair complexion, Cyn guessed, she would have seen a bright-red blush, but on Jericho it was more like the ghost of a blush. It flashed under his dark skin and an embarrassed smile flickered through his eyes and was gone.

Jericho coughed, paid for the drinks, apologized for making a mess, and gestured for Cyn to lead as they headed back toward her waiting laptop.

Cyn took a long sip of her gloriously hot latte and licked the milk froth from her top lip, blushing a little when Jericho's eyes fixated on her mouth. She hadn't meant to do that. Well, maybe she had. *My emotions are getting out of control,* she warned herself, terrified that letting her guard down with Jericho would let the "too much" boil over.

"Chai?" she asked, a teasing light flickering in her eyes. "That's a bit unexpected."

Jericho dropped his black Stetson on the table and brushed a speck of non-existent dirt from the brim.

Letting him off the hook, Cyn smiled and confessed, "I love real chai, but it's rare to find it in a coffee shop. Is the stuff here good?"

"It's not homemade," Jericho said, finally looking up from the spotless hat. He sipped the savoury chai slowly and gave a deep, relaxed breath. "But it hits the spot. Aditi taught me to make Chai last year. I met her and Devan when she came from England for Founder's Day. She was in one of the classes at the high school talking about some of her family's customs and cultural food."

"You went to Peace High School?" Cyn was confused. She had deliberately forgotten a lot about her high school years, but Jericho she would have remembered. "I never ran into you."

"It was last summer," he explained. "I was there doing some repairs. They needed some roof work done and the budget had been cut to the point where the school couldn't pay for it." He shrugged. "It wasn't a big deal, but it was a cool day and so when Aditi brought a chai out to me, I fell in love."

"Oh." Cyn's voice went lifeless and flat. She hardly knew Jericho, but the idea of him falling in love with someone bothered her, really bothered her. Red flags started waving in the part of Cyn's mind that was determined to stay detached, to care about nothing and no one except her mom.

"Yes!" he exclaimed. "I loved it so much that I talked Aditi into giving me the recipe and helping me buy a spice grinder." He looked down embarrassedly. "I keep it hidden in the horse barn." A rueful smile ran across his face. "I'm just not social enough to share, and I don't want the guys making fun."

"I understand that completely," Cyn agreed. "I've always been a bit of an outcast in Peace. We moved here when I was in grade nine and even though my mom grew up here, that makes me a stranger."

Lunch time came and went as they chatted, the sun sparkled through the windows with their bright holiday decorations. Cyn kept shaking her head internally, she just couldn't believe that she was talking to a cowboy, a horse breaker. Biting her lip and giving an unintentional tug on her dark braid, Cyn listened as Jericho talked and talked. They covered everything from their favourite music—his was classical, hers indie-folk—opinions on world politics, and their hopes for life in Peace. Jericho The Quiet was a garrulous soul once he started.

Cyn even told him about her dwindling hopes for college. How her dream of becoming a "real" doctor had seemed so close when she was accepted into the Psych program at Montana State University but was now rapidly drowning under her mom's medical issues and the ever-increasing pile of bills. "I've got a full-ride scholarship starting in the spring, but how can I take it. I couldn't I leave mom to handle it all alone. It's hard not to feel angry," she admitted, giving the errant braid a hard pull. "But how can I begrudge it, when it's saving Mom's life." Clouds drifted through the depths of Cyn's berry-brown eyes as she thought about the uncertainty around her future. "How could I be such an awful person?"

She was cut short as Jericho reached across the small cafe table to gently tuck her braid back behind her, stopping her agitated tugs. His hand was warm against her chin as he tilted her face up to meet his eyes. "Stop it," he said. His dark eyes met her warm brown ones only to drop away quickly. "Are you stopping your mom from getting treatment?"

"Of course not!" Cyn's response was outraged,

"I'd do anything to get Mom well again!"

"Do you think your mom wants you to lose this chance at your future," he asked.

"I haven't told her about the scholarship," Cyn admitted, "It would be cruel to put that kind of guilt trip on her."

"Then you are not a horrible person, Cyn." Jericho's thumb ghosted across her lips and down her cheek. "You are, in fact, quite wonderful." Jericho's hand dropped from her face and he leaned back, long denim-covered legs stretched out under the table.

What do I do with a comment like that, Cyn thought, feeling the gentle caress long after Jericho had looked away, once again becoming fascinated with the imaginary lint on his hat.

Her fingers tapped nervously on the top of her closed laptop. It wasn't the first compliment she had ever had, but it was the least expected.

"I'm sorry, Miss Cynthia," he said, picking up his hat and looking at the door. "That was very forward of me." The quiet Jericho was back, face closed and eyes shuttered. Cyn felt like she had been standing in front of an open door only to have it close in her face, leaving her outside in the storm. She missed the chatterbox Jericho. *He's shy,* she realized. *This big, smart cowboy is just shy!*

Glancing at her watch, Cyn was surprised to find that it was after 3:30. They had been there for almost four hours! "Crap," she exclaimed. "I have to go back to the hotel—my mom will be done at the library soon and I need to grab the car and pick her up." She smiled warmly, trying to melt the distance behind Jericho's eyes. "I'm so glad we ran into each other, Jericho. This has been one of my best afternoons in a long time."

That brought Jericho's quiet smile back. "Would you let me walk you back to the hotel?" he asked, picking up his hat and shrugging into the warm black duster.

Cyn bit her lip and then giggled. "I was hoping you would offer," she said. "I don't know Helena all that well, and I'm afraid I'd get turned around." Packing up her laptop and shoving her arms in her black pea-coat, she got ready for the November cold. Jericho tipped his hat to the blue-eyed cashier and, pointedly taking Cyn's hand, followed Cyn out onto the street.

"Where are you staying?" he asked. "I'm at the Baymont."

"Us too!" Cyn glanced down at their joined hands, tan against black. It felt warm and safe—it felt more than that. "Would you like to join me and my mom for dinner later?" Cyn couldn't believe she'd been brave enough to ask, but she just wanted to keep that warm light in his eyes. "That's supposing Mama feels well enough to eat."

Another of those not-blushes crept up Jericho's cheeks. "I'd love to join you, Miss Cynthia. Thank you so much for asking."

The November sun was setting as they settled

down in the Melaque Mexican Restaurant. Wafts of heat and incredible smells came from the kitchen every time a waiter carried food to a table and the restaurant was full of the clatter of friendly people and the occasional shout of "winner" from the casino next door. Cyn was amazed. Her usually quiet mother had charmed Jericho out of his boots. She had him telling stories about his childhood in the south, discussing the power shift in town since Dexie McBride arrived and overturned the status quo, and talking about his plans to build a permanent home in Peace. *He looks so good,* Cyn thought, *laughing and joking with Mom.* The white button-down shirt he wore emphasized the breadth of his chest and highlighted the flash of his teeth when his rare smile peeped out. *It's strange,* she mused. *Suddenly, I'm the quiet one.* Mom and Jericho were talking like they had known each other forever and a small, unwelcome part of Cyn's mind rumbled with something that tasted a bit like jealousy.

They ate deep-fried, Mexican ice-cream and talked until Bev's shoulders started to droop, then walked slowly back to the hotel, Jericho with one arm around Cyn's shoulders and a strong hand at Bev's waist, just in case. He said it was to make sure they didn't slip. Cyn didn't care, Jericho was a warm solid presence beside her in the dark. His hand brushed her hair. She'd worn it loose for a change, and when the wind whipped it around her shoulders, he gently tucked the dark silk in behind her ear. *For months,* Cyn thought, *I've tried to be the rock that held our world together, through the cancer diagnosis, Brent's death, and the upheavals that his death had caused in Peace.* Then Mom's decision to close down the clinic, everything seemed to be landing on her.

She had tried to stand on her own so that she wouldn't add a feather's weight to the burdens her mother carried.

Now, for the first time, she felt that there might be someone she could lean on. They said goodnight in the reception area of the hotel and headed to their rooms. Cyn just couldn't help it— she turned her head to steal a glance behind her, not really knowing what she was looking for. What she saw set her heart racing. Jericho was leaning on the front desk of the hotel and watching her with such a lost look in his eyes that, had her mother not opened the hotel room and turned the lights on at that exact moment, Cyn may have turned back. *And who knows,* she thought regretfully, *what would have happened then.*

Chapter 4

They didn't see Jericho the next morning. Bev didn't sleep well and Cyn wanted to get her back to her own bed. So Cyn packed up before dawn and loaded everything into the POS Prius and they headed back to Peace.

"I need to talk to you, little bird," Bev commented after they'd been on the road for a while. She didn't turn around to look at Cyn as she spoke but gazed at the passing grasslands while her hands twisted around each other.

"What is it, Mama?" Cyn asked, taking one hand off the wheel to place them over Bev's gloved hands. "Something is bothering you, that's obvious! You haven't called me little bird since I was a kid, and you won't even look at me."

"I need to tell you something, Cyn, and I'm not sure how to start, but you need to know."

"Is this about that case that was worrying you?" Cyn prodded. Reaching over she turned the heating in the car up a few notches. Bev's skin looked pale under the knitted cap she had pulled over her short regrowth of brown hair. She had found this winter hard, the chemo had taken so much strength, but as the doctors kept saying, it was worth it if the cancer was in remission.

"In part." Bev's dark eyes were solemn, the normal twinkle banked down to an ember. "Can we pull over somewhere quiet, just for a few minutes?"

Cyn's heart pounded. *What now? The cancer? The clinic?* She couldn't remember the last time her mom had sounded so serious, almost scared.

Cyn pulled off the highway and into the empty parking lot of the Skidway Campground on Route 12. Throwing the car into park she turned to face her mother, worried by the quiet, unsure tone of voice. "Mama?"

The road through the Helena National Forest was quiet, the normally bustling campground closed for the winter. But everything, the crisp air, the mountains, the beautiful scenery, was all lost on Cyn. She saw nothing but her mom's strained face. "What the heck is going on?"

Digging through the tattered black briefcase, Bev pulled out a folded wad of paper. Smoothing them out, she sighed deeply and turned to face Cyn. "I need to make a decision, Cyn, but the effects of it will not just fall on me, it will be your life too that could change, and not necessarily for the better." Cyn's eyebrows shot up. Unbuckling her seatbelt, she twisted around to stare at her mom. The steering wheel dug sharply into her side, but she didn't notice.

"You're confusing me," she said, sounding much younger than her twenty-six years. "Please stop."

Bev pulled her red, knitted hat further down

around her freezing ears and coughed. "Did you know that part of a counsellor's responsibility is to report to the police if you think a client is planning to harm themselves or someone else?"

"I didn't," Cyn said, her mind running through her mother's innocuous list of clients. Could one of them be dangerous? Did Peace have any security companies that could put alarms on the trailer? "Should I be worried?"

"Stop talking and listen," Bev said, her tone growing stronger now that she had started talking. "I've had to call the police on clients a time or two, but it's the second part of the law that I'm worried about right now. The part you don't normally run into in practice. You have to report a client that is going to commit a crime, but what if the crime is already done? Does that fall under privileged information, since no one is at risk?" Bev covered her eyes, then peeked over the top of her hand like a child playing peekaboo. "This is what I need to decide." She counted off points on her bony fingers as she spoke, taking a moment to wave them in front of the heater vent.

"Do I report this client who has admitted to committing a serious crime. If I do, that might be a breach of confidence and potentially cost me my licence. Also, if I bring the crime to the police, there will be an investigation and the publicity, honestly, will be awful. Or should I keep my peace, muzzle my conscience, and trust it when this client says that they will never offend again?"

Cyn's mind was a whirl of uncontrollable

thoughts, the most vocal one being, *Who?* "I can't tell you what to do, Momma. But it scares me. Either way, it scares me."

"I know, little bird." Bev's small hand rested on her leg for a moment before fluttering back to the heating vent. "I haven't decided, and it's a hell of a lot more complex than I've said, but I have to act soon. For now, let's get home. I'm freezing, and my heart is sore."

Cyn leaned over to wrap an arm around her mom. "I trust you, Mom. Just don't blindside me, please. Let me know if something is going to come at me."

"I swear, little bird," Bev said, taking Cyn's long-fingered hand in hers. "I will tell you as much as I can, and honey," she said, pulling the woolen hat back onto her head and wrapping her arms around her chest, tucking her hands into the sleeves of her parka, "I'm scared too."

Neither of them spoke as Cyn pulled the car back onto the highway, headed for Peace. *God,* she thought, *that name has never been so misleading.*

Chapter 5

And so, November passed in a swirl of snowflakes and preoccupation. Thanksgiving crept up without Cyn noticing until she was blindsided when Bev insisted that she attend the town Thanksgiving dinner on the Friday before the holiday.

"Mama, I'm staying home, and that's it!" Cyn tried to keep her voice gentle and patient when she really wanted to shout in anger. Her mother had been bugging her about going to the town's Thanksgiving Dinner ever since they got home from the clinic today. "I don't have a date, and I'm not going to sit on my own looking pathetic."

"Now, little bird," her mother's use of her family name had Cyn rolling her eyes. When that name came out it was always something "for her own good." Cyn sat down heavily on the threadbare flowered couch. While the clinic got the best of everything, there often wasn't enough left over for luxuries at home—new furniture, or repairs for their clanky old Prius, always had to wait.

"I promised Dexie that we would be at the Thanksgiving Dinner. It's the first time the town has held a charity fundraiser like this since Brent Harrington got it cancelled years back because of 'budget shortfalls.'" Beverley snorted indelicately, a loud humphing noise quite out of keeping with the frail afghan-wrapped woman in her wicker rocking chair. "More like he found out that there wasn't any money the Harringtons could skim from the event. In any case," Bev's voice hardened, "I told Dexie that we would be there. I swore to myself that I would help this hellhole of a town move past what the Harringtons have done to it over the last 60 years. And since *I* can't be, *you* will be! Now get dressed and go represent this family."

Cyn walked into the high school gymnasium a few hours later, the points of her burgundy patchwork dress brushing her long legs with every step she took. Smiling at Dray and Dexie as they took their places at the head table, she slipped into her seat, eyes shining sadly as she noticed the place card for Dr. Beverley Redman still sitting at the empty seat next to hers.

Mom would have loved this, Cyn thought, looking around the gymnasium, which was festooned with orange and bronze harvest streamers and oversized cut-outs of cartoonish turkeys. A large wicker cornucopia occupied the table near the door and many of the more affluent residents stopped on their way in to drop money, vouchers for food or Christmas toys, or other gifts that would be shared among the less fortunate in Peace. *This is what this town can be,* Cyn thought.

Not just the grasping, fearful place I grew up in, but a real community.

David Falton, breath reeking of beer, spun the chair next to Cyn around and planted himself in it, long arms dangling over the chair back. "Hey, pretty gal," he said, belching yeastily. His rough hand brushed Cyn's arm as he reached to play with the dark braid trailing over her bare shoulder. "You sure dress up pretty, even though your hair still makes you look like a squaw."

Cyn pushed her chair back until it crashed into the gymnasium wall. "Mr. Falton," she hissed. "Please keep your hands, and your comments, to yourself!"

When Cyn started junior high in Peace, most of her schoolmates hadn't even mentioned her native bloodlines. Classes, homework, and pop music had been much more important. But David had never missed a chance to remind her that she was an outsider, a half-breed. His rough hands would yank on her braid whenever she walked past him, and *squaw* was one of the nicer things he had called her. Her mom had said that he liked her, in an immature and boorish way. Cyn didn't believe it then. She still didn't believe it.

"David, get the hell away from me." She spoke a bit louder this time, causing a few heads to turn.

"Aww come on, Cyn." David pulled his chair closer to her, effectively trapping her between the gym wall and the banquet tables. "You're here alone." Again, his hand grabbed at her braid, trailing the loose ends over the hint of cleavage exposed by the sweetheart neckline of her dress. "We could dump this place and go find some real fun."

Grabbing at the first thing she could reach on the table, Cyn threw it straight in David's face. Instantly, he pulled away, madly grabbing for napkins from the table, anything to blot the purple-something punch from his no-doubt rented tux.

"I won't forget this, you ungrateful bitch!" he blustered. "I've got friends in this town." He loomed over Cyn as she tried to edge past him, wishing mightily for her runners instead of the useless red heels. David yelped as someone yanked him back across the banquet table and, with a swift punch to the jaw, dumped him unceremoniously on the dance floor.

Completely ignoring the moaning and threats coming from where David lay on the floor, as well as the stares from everyone around them, Jericho held out a hand to Cynthia, tucking her arm under his, they walked towards the gym door.

"Are you okay, Miss Cynthia?" Jericho asked once they'd reached a quieter area, away from the hoopla in the gym. "Did that son of a..."—he swallowed and coughed—"'scuse me, ma'am..."

Cyn laughed delightedly, suddenly believing that this evening might be worth the hassle of dressing up. "You were right with the first description," she said, her dark eyes sparkling. "I've never had a knight in wrangler armour before." The burgundy tails of her dress dipped as Cyn curtsied awkwardly. "My thanks, kind sir."

Jericho tipped his black "dressed-up" Stetson and flashed her one of his rare smiles. "I'm just glad I was here to help, Miss Cynthia," he said, looking over her shoulder and back into the gymnasium where David was showing off his ruined suit jacket and telling anyone who would listen how unstable and vindictive she was.

"Well, there goes any hope I had of getting a scholarship from this town. Miss Congeniality, I'm not." Cyn screwed her mouth into a wry smirk. "I never did have the patience to put up with his kind of horse-crap."

Jericho kicked the toe of his worn boots against the wall. "Well, Miss Cynthia. I don't know about his horse-crap, but do you think you could put up with mine? Enough to go for a drive or something this weekend?"

It had been so long since anyone had asked her out that Cyn just froze, staring at Jericho.

"I'm sorry, ma'am." Jericho started to turn back to the gym. "I shouldn't have mentioned anything, not when you've been hassled already tonight."

Cyn reached out and grabbed his hand, determined to stop him, her pale fingers looking ghostly against his strong, dark arm. "You are the best part of tonight." Her eyes flashed past his briefly, not long enough to be called a glance, but definitely enough time for both to feel the sparks jump between them.

"I would love to go for a drive with you, when you have time of course."

Jericho's strong hand tipped her head up, forcing her to meet the depths of his eyes. "May I call for you on Saturday then?" His mouth was saying words, she heard them, but her eyes fixated on his lips, strong and masculine with just a hint of softness. *I could stay here forever,* she thought, not listening, just staring.

"Miss Cynthia?" he asked. And when she didn't answer, "Cyn?"

"Oh." Cyn pulled herself out of her daydreams. "Saturday would be perfect. Around 2 p.m.?" she added. "And please, Jericho, call me Cynthia. I like the way you say it."

"Should we go back in?" he asked, nodding in the direction of the gymnasium. David Falton was standing just inside the double doors, rubbing his jaw and watching Jericho intently. "Or have you had enough of this place for one night?"

"For one night?" Cyn answered. "I've had enough of Peace for a lifetime." She shrugged. "Not all of Peace," she admitted glancing over her shoulder at David's hate-filled face. "Just parts of it."

"I won't forget this, Matthews." David's voice was loud and harsh. His words slurred by anger, beer, and a jaw that was turning purple enough to match the stains on his shirt. "You hear me, you bastard? No one messes with me and gets away with it."

"He's drunk," Cyn said, turning away from the unpleasant sight. "David has been a bully since junior high. He's just spouting." Carefully examining her burgundy sandals, Cyn swallowed thickly and spoke in a rush. "Would you like to grab a drink and sit somewhere quiet? I don't want to go back in there, but I can't leave yet. Mama told me that I had to stay for the speeches."

"That sounds great, Cynthia." Jericho made the long form of her name sound so special. "I'll grab us some punch and be back in a minute. Think about where we can go to hide."

A few minutes later, paper cups in hand, Cyn and Jericho wandered around the hallways looking for a place to sit. Jericho pushed on the crash-bar that opened the front stairwell and they both laughed as two red-faced teenagers broke apart and scuttled quickly up to the second floor. "Maybe this isn't a good place." Cyn laughed. Finally settling down on the padded bench in front of the principal's office, Cyn played idly with the floating edges of her dress. Jericho's eyes followed her movements and she saw a small flame jump to life as she smoothed the burgundy fabric over her knees. *I'm flirting with him*, she thought, astonished at her own behaviour. *What the hell do I think I'm doing?*

Whatever it was, it worked, because a moment later Jericho's dark hand—nails short and cracked, but impeccably clean—followed the path that her hand had taken over her knee and down to where the hem of her dress lay draped across her leg. "So soft," he whispered. His wandering hand now cupping her cheek, his thumb gently stroked along her high cheekbones. "I knew that your skin would be the softest thing I'd ever touched."

Sliding his hand into the hair at the back of her neck, he angled her head down toward his, eyes fascinated by her lips. "Miss Cynthia, may I..."

Cyn had had enough of waiting for her southern gentleman, leaning in she closed the gap between their lips. Closing her eyes and letting go of all the reasons she shouldn't be doing this, she gave herself to this moment, and to Jericho. His lips were firm and soft, the hand against her cheek felt callused, but not rough. He gently explored the contours of her face, shooting fireworks through her heart and, as he pulled her closer, warming her body until it melted against his. Her hands wandered, almost instinctively, over the muscled outlines of his chest, delighting in the contrast between the soft denim shirt and the hot, hard man who wore it. Jericho growled softly, nipping at her lips in appreciation. She sighed, opening further to him, asking, although she didn't quite know what for.

He knew. His hand grasped her head tighter and his agile tongue slipped between her lips to stroke the roof of her mouth. One large hand cupped her breast, the soft weight no more than a palmful for the big cowboy. She gasped when his thumb brushed lightly over her nipple, making it pebble tightly beneath the soft chiffon.

The giggles of a couple of teenagers shattered their privacy. Jericho and Cyn looked at each other with embarrassment, recognizing the same young couple that they had chased out of the stairwell earlier. "Cynthia, I…"

Cyn put a shushing finger over his lips. "Shush, Jericho," she said quietly, nodding at the pair of teenagers peering through the windows of the stairwell door. "I think we've given them quite enough to talk about for now."

"I'm sorry." Jericho sounded contrite, but his hand was still entwined with hers, his thumb still brushing small caresses over the sensitive skin of her wrist, sending shivers through her system, leaving Cyn to wonder how far things might have gone. She would never know. Although reliving the scene later that night, she hoped that she would have had the sense to stop…maybe.

Walking back into the gymnasium a few minutes later, Cyn felt like she had been thrown into a whirlwind. Her ears ached with all the noise, and the people seemed to push against her from every side despite Jericho's formidable bulk creating a barrier between her and the crowd.

Everyone was dancing or talking and seemed to be having fun, but after the quiet intimacy of before it seemed overwhelming. Looking up at Jericho, Cyn smiled gently. "I should get home," she said. "Mama will be worried if I'm too late, and I don't think anything happening here can compete with what was the best part of my evening."

"Are we still going driving on Saturday?" Jericho asked, his voice diffident, letting her set the pace. He didn't let go of her hand though, making sure that everyone, especially David Falton, saw that they were together.

"I'll meet you at two," Cyn confirmed. "I have to do some paperwork at the clinic on Saturday morning, so why don't we meet up at Generic Eric's?"

"Sure." Jericho smiled happily, kissing her hand before he let it go. "Wear something warm— we might go for a walk."

Cyn turned to go without noticing that at the back of the gym David Falton watched, his eyes bright with unblinking menace.

Chapter 6

"Why did you bring me out here, Jericho?" Cyn was confused—this was hardly typical first-date territory. The empty land stretched out in front of Cyn, miles of cattle land. Rolling hills, scrub and meadows stretching south toward town. From here, only the pinnacle of the Catholic church could be seen. Peace was, literally and figuratively, miles away.

"I wanted you to see something that's special to me," Jericho said. "We're almost there now." The paved road had turned into gravel a few miles back, and now the gravel turned to dirt and the old truck shuddered to a stop out on a bluff overlooking Peace Valley.

"This is the most beautiful piece of land I've ever seen," Jericho said, looking around with a kind of wonder.

Climbing out of the beat-up Ford, she shaded her eyes. "It's pretty," she said, kind of prodding Jericho to fill in the rest of his thoughts.

"There's good water here, grazing land for easily a hundred head of horses, but the amazing part is this. Close your eyes, Cynthia."

With her eyes closed, and Jericho's hands warm on her shoulders, Cyn had trouble even thinking, never mind listening for whatever she was supposed to hear. Jericho turned her around again. The sound of the running water told her that she was facing out over the bluff toward the distant Rockies. "Just listen," he said.

Slowing her breathing and calming her racing heart wasn't easy with his hands warm and strong on her arms, but finally Cyn heard it. The swoosh noise of the November wind through the dead leaves, the sluggish burble of the creek as the water pushed around the rapidly forming ice and over all the silence. A silence that was so heavy it had a weight and texture of its own.

"I wanted this place for the silence," Jericho whispered. "I've never been anywhere that the quiet had a kind of feeling. I'm planning on building here," he said. "I've already set up a corral for a few of my horses down by the road." He pointed to an old farmhouse in the copse near the road. Bales of hay stacked by the broken-down door showed that no matter how forlorn the building looked, it was in use. From inside Cyn could hear the *whuff* of horses breathing in the cold fresh air.

"The old owners had their house down there," Jericho said, turning her away from the barn. "But my house is going to be up here." Jericho gestured toward the edge of the bluff. "Where I can hear the wind." He smiled at Cyn. "I'm hoping to start building in Spring. The town services already come to the main road here and it wouldn't take much to get them trenched out to the bluff. It will take a while to get it done, but I think working on days off and such I can do this." Jericho sounded so free and happy when he talked about his place. Cyn watched the dreams dance in his eyes and wondered if there would be some place for her on his bluff.

"Do you want to meet my horses?" Jericho asked diffidently. Taking her by the hand, he led her down to the half-broken door of the old farmhouse. The warm smell of horses and straw made Cyn's nose wrinkle up and she inhaled it deeply. Most of the stalls were empty but the ones furthest away from the door and the wind held two beautiful horses that raised their heads and looked at them with intelligent eyes as they entered. *It looks bigger on the inside,* Cyn thought, then giggled at herself for the unintentional reference. But it was true. Jericho had gutted the inside of the old farmhouse and built large stalls down the length of the main floor.

Jericho handed her a grain bag and she approached the first stall. "This is Cleo," Jericho said, laying a gentle hand on the horse's head. "Her full name is Cleopatra of the West, but that's a mouthful."

Extending her hand to the mare, Cyn felt the gentlest touch imaginable as the horse's lips scraped her hand clean. "She's beautiful," Cyn whispered, feeding another handful of grain to her majesty, Queen Cleopatra. The dark head of the horse in the second stall turned toward her voice and a loud whicker let her know that Cleo had had her share of the attention. "And who do we have over here," Cyn said, offering a flat palm to the horse and giggling when its warm breath tickled.

"His name is Argo," Jericho informed her. "Watch him—he's a bit skittish. I bought him at a police sale, and he'd been roughly used."

"Who would abuse such a gorgeous creature!" Cyn's eyes flashed and her voice rose with indignation, startling Argo, who pranced backwards and whinnied loudly. "Oh Argo, I'm sorry," Cyn apologized in a singsong tone that cajoled the frightened animal into coming back for his turn at the feed bag.

With a final pat on the muzzle, Cyn said goodbye to Argo and turned back to Jericho. "Although I like to think I'm a bit more 'citified' than the typical yokel in Peace," she said with a self-deprecating shrug, "put me out here, and I guess I'm just a cowgirl."

Something lost and lonely drifted through Jericho's dark eyes. "Let's get outside," he said unexpectedly, then shouldered his way past Cyn and headed out the open doorway.

Cyn quickly closed the door to the old house and followed Jericho down the hill. *What did I do,* she worried, *is he angry because I startled Argo?*

Jericho didn't turn around as she approached him. He stood facing out over the bluff staring at the river. "Jericho?" Cyn's voice seemed to snap him out of his funk and he turned to look at her.

"What's wrong?" Cyn asked. "I'm sorry if I frightened Argo, I didn't mean to."

Jericho reached out a dark hand and touched her arm gently, "I wasn't mad at you Cynthia," he explained rubbing the sleeve of his denim jacket over suspiciously bright eyes. "I've just never had someone I cared for who understood and loved my horses too. It shook me, Cyn."

Jericho turned away his glance roaming from the bluff where they stood to the old farmhouse and further out to the distant mountains. "My horses are the only things I've ever dared to love." He turned back to her slowly, tipping her chin up so that she could see his eyes clearly, their warm depths filled with unashamed tears. "Until now," he said his thumb drifting over her slightly parted lips. "This place was supposed to be my haven, my Peace," he confessed. "Now, out of nowhere, my peace is wrapped up in a little gal with wounded eyes and a voice that whispers to the wild in my soul."

Jericho's hand slowly drifted over her head, tangling in Cyn's dark braid, pulling her towards him. "You move me." His lips settled over hers, light as a butterfly's wings, not demanding, just sipping gently. *He tastes like tears,* Cyn thought dropping her head into the crook of his shoulder, certain that she could feel her heart breaking. *I've gone over the edge,* she admitted to herself. *He matters-he wasn't supposed to matter.*

A terrified whinny pulled them apart and sent Jericho racing up the hill toward the horses. Smoke billowed from the hay bales stacked up for insulation along the outside walls of the old farmhouse. Cyn could hear the horses kicking madly at the wooden walls desperate to escape the smoke.

"Stay there, Cyn," Jericho bellowed at her over his shoulder. Pulling his jacket off and wrapping it around his head, he dashed into the thick smoke, headed toward the panicking horses.

Cyn watched him disappear into the smoke. *Please, God, no,* she thought, *I can't lose him.* Grabbing her old flip-phone from her jeans pocket she punched in the only number her scrambled brain could remember. "Mom," she spoke hurriedly. "Call the fire department and the sheriff and get them up to Jericho Matthews place off Oak Road. We've got a barn fire!"

"Please, Jericho," she muttered hanging up the phone. "Please! I can't lose you!"

Heart pounding, breath coming in painful gasps, Cyn ran toward the road. *They will be here soon,* she thought, *they have to be!* Breaking through the screen of trees that separated the bluff from Oak Road, Cyn was almost run over as a black Dodge Durango crashed out of the bushes and barrelled down the road toward town.

David! She cursed, recognizing the square head with its shaggy blond hair. The faint sound of sirens in the direction of town interrupted her cursing. Help was coming.

The volunteer fire brigade pulled up and swung into action. The 4-x-4's forced a path through the scrub until they could drop their hoses into the creek and start pumping water onto the now fully involved corral.

"Jericho," Cyn yelled frantically, only to see him emerge leading Cleo, the gentle silver palomino that she had been feeding earlier. The horse had Jericho's sheepskin jacket wrapped tightly over it's eyes, taking away the terrifying image of flames, and it followed Jericho's voice docilely, trusting the deep slow voice to lead her out of the dark. "I got them both," he coughed, ignoring the raw red burns on his hands and arms. "Argo is safe too."

Sirens again, a different pitch this time though. Cyn recognized the Sheriff's vehicle before Dray even stepped out.

"Jericho? Cyn? You okay?" His grey eyes flashed around the scene, professional suspicion fighting with his obvious concern.

"Not sure what happened, Dray," Jericho said between coughing fits. "The hay bales caught fire—I don't know how. I got the stock out, but the corral is a write off."

A medic from the fire department approached Jericho, but Jericho shrugged him off.

"Are you okay, Cyn?" he said. "I'm sorry our day was ruined like this."

"It was David." Cyn turned to face Dray, shoulders high, voice cracking with fury. "I saw him pull out of the bush when I ran out to flag you down."

"That's a serious accusation, Cyn," Dray said. "Are you sure?"

"It was David," she repeated. "His Durango is unmistakable."

"Show me where he pulled out of the bush," Dray ordered, his face stern and professional.

Walking back toward the road, Cyn pointed out where the big truck had crashed through the underbrush and the black marks on the asphalt where it had peeled out and rushed past her.

"Yep." Dray bent over looking at the tracks in the soft ground. "It was David. He's the only one in town with the military-grade run-flat tires—see those hatch marks in the tire treads?" Walking back to his jeep, Dray pulled out a digital camera and started taking pictures. The scorched corral, the hay bales, the tire tracks and the road, everything was documented. Grabbing the mic on his dash, he hailed the station. "This is Sheriff Palmer. First, I need a forensic team out from Billings, get them here before the snow falls." Dray glanced at the sky with the practised eye of an outdoorsman. "They've got two hours. Until they get here, I need that new deputy. What's his name again? I don't know, Deputy Donut, just get him, out here to guard the site. Oh, and call Dr. Vetani, we've got injured horses, they'll be at my place in about an hour. Also, I need a squad car to pick up David Falton and bring him in for questioning—suspected arson." Cyn heard a mumble of assent on the other side of the radio and a few words of random instructions, then Dray was straightening up out of the jeep to turn around and face Jericho.

"It's over, Jericho." Cyn's hand rested on the arm of Jericho's flannel shirt. Even now she couldn't ignore how nice the soft fabric felt over the hardness of his muscles. "Let the medic look at your hands. There's nothing else to do here."

Jericho smiled, a sooty-faced, red-eyed smile that tried to be reassuring but just wasn't. "I need to see to the horses, Cyn." He shrugged, flinching as his movements pulled on the angry burns covering his hands and forearms.

"Rusty is on his way from the ranch," Dray interrupted. He'll take your horses down to the McBride farm. We'll keep them until you get the corral re-done or a barn up. For now, let them see to your damn burns and then take Cyn home. Dexie has a new mare coming in tomorrow and she'll need you at work."

"Yes, sir," Jericho submitted less-than-gracefully, finally allowing the hovering medic to bandage his hands and forearms. "I need to check on the horses for myself before we leave," he protested. "I'm not sure if they were injured."

Cyn tugged on his uninjured arm, directing him toward the old truck. "Dr. Vetani will meet Rusty at the McBride's. I heard Dray arrange it when he called the station."

Chapter 7

When Cyn woke up on the Thursday after Thanksgiving to find her mom gone and a note stuck to the fridge that read *Had an appointment early—see you at the clinic*, she panicked. *Not again!* Cyn grumbled, clattering around the kitchen of the old trailer. *This is the third time she's just disappeared since we went to Helena. It's just not like her to go out without telling me where she is or when she'll be back.*

Hands tightening on the old checkered towel she was using to dry her breakfast dishes, Cyn carefully stacked her bowl in the cupboard and wished her mom was there to hear the door slam. *Well, wondering where Mom has gone isn't productive,* she thought. *I need to get to the clinic. Then when she comes in,* Cyn promised herself, *I'll find a way to force her to talk to me.*

Leaning out the front door to start the car, and hastily shoving her hair into a sloppy braid, Cyn grabbed her coat and purse and stepped out into the cold. As she pulled out of their parking stall, Peace's only snow plow, an ancient yellow machine driven by whichever member of the volunteer fire department wasn't working, trundled past the entrance to the mobile home park, black clouds of diesel smoke trailing in its wake. Idling the motor while she waited for it to pass, Cyn silently blessed her mom's mechanic, who had installed an auto starter for her when he found out that Bev was ill. On mornings like this, the warmth felt so good!

Waiting for the turn light on Oak Street seemed to take ages. Cyn bopped her head in time to the radio and watched as two elderly residents walked carefully down the street toward the all-night gas station. *Probably going to pick up lottery cards,* she thought. *Maybe that's what I need to do. I can't see any other way that I'll ever be able to get to college.* With all the medical bills, neither Bev nor Cyn had been able to take a salary from the clinic for months. They'd been living off their dwindling savings, and that wasn't going to go much further.

The sound of Queen's *Bohemian Rhapsody* shattered her thoughts. "Mom," she said, thumbing her cell phone to speaker. "Where the heck are you?"

"This is not a good connection." Bev's voice, echoing through the small speaker on her Nokia flip-phone, sounded tinny and far away. "I had to go to Billings for an appointment, Cyn. I'll be on my way back in a few hours. Please have everything ready for my one o'clock client. I'll be in well before he arrives."

"Billings?" Cyn pulled the hated blue Prius into the back of the clinic and threw it agitatedly into park. "Mama, what on earth are you doing there without me?" *Something must be seriously wrong,* Cyn thought, her stomach twisting with anxiety. Consciously relaxing her death grip on the phone, she tried to swallow around a lump that tasted almost like betrayal. Cyn had gone everywhere, done everything with Bev for the last year, ever since the diagnosis. *I should be happy,* she told herself. *I'm supposed to be glad that Mom is out and doing things on her own again.* But she wasn't. Was this the doctors? Something about the patient issue that Mama was dealing with? Whatever it was, it was just one more secret, one more thing for Cyn to worry about.

"Gotta go," Bev said. "I'll be back for my one o'clock." Then the phone disconnected abruptly, and just like that, Cyn was sitting in the parking lot, alone. Climbing out into the slush, Cyn slammed the door in aggravation, then apologized to the old car and promised that she would never abuse the hinges again, as long as it kept working.

Bev walked in a few hours later, her hair spiky from the wind and her face looking tired and pale. "The bus ride was awful," she said, wrapping her cold arms around Cyn. Giving Cyn an apologetic hug, she made her careful way to the back room.

"Are you going to…"

"No." Bev cut her off before she could demand explanations.

"Mama, I was worried about you. It's not fair that you just disappear like that!" Cyn's voice crackled with anger and her slight shoulders hunched aggressively.

"I'm not a child, Cynthia," Bev said in a tone that Cyn called her Doctor Redman Voice. "Just because I've needed some help—and I appreciate it, truly—doesn't mean that I can't take a bus on my own. I'm your mother, not the other way around."

"You wouldn't know that from the way things have been this year," Cyn muttered under her breath. *Why am I so angry?* she thought. *Mama is doing better—I should be throwing a party.*

Bev smiled. One of those "I'm the counsellor" smiles that drove Cyn crazy.

"Don't," Cyn warned flashing a withering glare at her mom. "Now isn't a good time for you to tell me all the reasons why I'm feeling this way and that it will all be okay." Cyn grabbed a random pile of paper from the reception desk and started staring at it as though it was the most fascinating thing she'd ever read. "Just don't."

"Send Mr. Jameson in when he gets here." Bev smiled quietly and walked into the therapy room. "We'll talk later. I do have news for you."

Cyn *hmphed* loudly. "After taking off three times for no apparent reason and then not saying a word when you came back? What if I don't want to listen?"

"Later," Bev said, "after you've stopped sulking because you aren't in charge anymore."

"I am not sulking," Cynthia retorted, but a part of her knew better. She'd done so much over the last year, sacrificed so much, a part of her didn't want to step back and be the daughter again.

Mr. Jameson showed up late, but that wasn't unusual for the laconic cowboy. He did some half-hearted flirting as he passed the reception desk and walked into the therapy room, closed the door, and started the session. Leaving Cyn with too much to think about and no answers.

Cyn's cell broke her introspective mood as it buzzed on her desk, making her jump. She grabbed it quickly so that it wouldn't disturb the session that had just started. The dark face and twinkling eyes that popped up on her screen instantly lifted her mood.

"Jericho," she said, moving swiftly into the back room. "I didn't think I'd hear from you today. How are your hands? How are the horses?"

Jericho's deep voice filled the office. "Not much for small talk, are you?" She could imagine him sitting in his old truck laughing at her.

Cyn blushed. She had never been good at "normal" talk. Her mouth filter just didn't work that way. "Sorry, Jericho." She smiled, knowing he really didn't mind that much. "It's been a bit of a morning and I'm not very social at the moment."

"Do you want me to call you later?" Jericho offered.

"Not at all." Cyn said, "Just hearing your voice has improved my mood tremendously. I had an argument with my mom." *It's nice to be able to say so,* she thought, shoulders slowly dropping as she relaxed, to have someone that she could talk to without filtering everything through what Mama needed.

"That must have been hard," he said. "I wish I was there, I could at least find a way to make you feel better."

"Oh," Cyn said curiously. "And how would you do that?"

"I would find a way." Jericho's voice dropped even lower, a note in his deep tone that had Cyn hoping her mom wouldn't come out of the session, at least for the next few minutes.

"Tell me," she said, wondering if he would be bold enough.

"Are you alone, my Cynthia?" Her heart started beating faster. Just the way he spoke her name held something warm and slightly dangerous. "Because if you were, I would back you up against your desk and kiss you until you forget why you were scared enough to argue with Bev."

Cynthia squirmed slightly, her body responding to the chocolate teasing.

"Then I would unbraid your hair, making it a cloak to cover your shoulders as I slowly pulled your shirt from your jeans so that I could warm your heart with my hands." Jericho's voice sounded strained, showing how much the imagery was affecting him. "Do you know what it does to me? Even thinking of holding the weight of you in my hands makes me hurt, my Cynthia. You make me feel like a teenager with his first gal."

"Am I?" Her voice was slightly breathless. "Your Cynthia?" She didn't normally play these games and it was affecting her more than she thought it would.

"You are mine, Cynthia Redman." Jericho's voice was quiet, almost understated. "Don't ever forget it; you are mine."

His words touched a warm place inside her, but a cold wind blew from her conflicted mind and pierced her heart. *What the hell am I doing* she thought, *egging him on, getting involved. I'm leaving in the Spring. He knows that M.S.U. agreed to delay my acceptance until for a term and that I still have the full scholarship available.*

"Jericho, I'm sorry. I should never have started this," Cyn admitted, taking several deep breaths to try and cool down. "It's unfair to both of us."

"Cynthia?" His voice came over the phone as a crackle of hurt. "Started what, Cyn? I can't read your mind. What are you trying to tell me?"

"I can't talk now," she replied, aching. "There are too many people around, too many things happening. But I'm not trying to play games or to hurt you. That's the last thing I want. I just..." Silent tears ran down her face. "I'll talk to you later. Please."

"Cynthia..." Jericho's voice sounded further away than ever. The distant, cautious Jericho was back. "I'll call for you tonight, if you wish."

"Let's have coffee at Generic Eric's," Cyn said, "and I'll try to explain things. It's just too confusing right now."

Jericho didn't sound convinced, but finally they agreed to meet at Generic Eric's at nine o'clock. Cyn was dreading it. Time to tell the truth.

Chapter 8

Generic Eric's was bustling when Cyn walked in at ten minutes to nine. *Not so busy,* she thought thankfully, *that I'll have to use the two-seater booth near the door.* Everyone knew that the table for that booth was off balance and would wobble if you didn't keep the food exactly in the middle. The waitresses had tried for years to balance it out, jamming things under the claw feet and adjusting the height—it didn't make a difference.

Sliding into one of the two-seater booths near the back of the diner, Cyn fidgeted nervously, wondering if, after her outburst this afternoon, Jericho would even show up. He did. The bells over the door jangled at exactly nine p.m., and there he was, walking through the door, black cowboy hat slammed low on his head, face impenetrable, eyes scanning the booths like beryl lasers. Spotting her, Jericho nodded curtly and slid in across the table.

The antique radio perched on the old counter belted out tinny Christmas music, perfectly matching the artificial wreath on the door and the spray-on snowmen decorating the large bank of windows facing main street.

"Hi," Jericho said, dropping his battered hat on the scuffed-up chrome-and-melamine tabletop. "I came."

"I wasn't sure you would," Cyn admitted. "I wouldn't have blamed you if you didn't want to speak to me after what happened this afternoon."

Tammy, the bottle-blonde waitress who had worked at Generic Eric's since Cyn was in high school, bustled up.

"Evening, Cyn, Jericho." She nodded, runaway curls bobbing around her heavily made-up face. "What can I get you kids tonight?" Tammy's faded hazel eyes twinkled with mischief, and you could almost hear her re-telling the story to the group of older ladies who came in for coffee every morning. *Jericho and Cynthia Redman? Interesting!*

After an awkward pause, they both ordered coffee and dessert and stared at the black-and-white tile floors, the chrome counters, anything but each other.

"So," Jericho finally opened the conversation once Tammy had dropped their coffees on the table and turned back to the front counter. "This afternoon..." His voice was calm, quiet, and distant enough to send a cold shiver crawling up Cyn's back.

"Let me talk, please," she asked, reaching across the table to put an admonitory hand on his arm. "This is hard and if I don't get it all out, I might lose my nerve."

Jericho leaned back, long legs stretched out under the table all the way to her side of the booth.

He didn't answer, just nodded and crossed his arms over his stomach, waiting.

"I...scared myself today, Jericho," Cyn explained "I realized how much I cared about you, how much I enjoyed what we were doing. It was too much. I...scared me."

Jericho's eyes didn't waver. "What did you expect?" he said full lips pursed. "To play around with the cowboy and not get involved?"

Cynthia dropped her head into her hands, massaging her temples, trying to get rid of the massive headache she felt building. "I don't know," she said. "I really don't know."

Not raising her eyes from where her hand was tracing idly over the pattern on the tabletop, she took a deep breath and blurted out the rest of her confession. "I've survived this year by not letting anyone else in. I couldn't afford to care about anyone but Mama." Cyn couldn't look at him, her eyes would say far more than she was willing to admit. "Before I met you, I knew exactly what I wanted."

Cyn fell quiet as the waitress slid a piece of deep-dish apple pie in front of her and handed pumpkin pie to Jericho, only continuing once she knew Tammy was gone.

"I was going to do whatever it took to see Mama through and then haul my ass out of this godforsaken town. I was going to college, getting a job at the hospital in Billings or Helena, and starting the life I'd dreamed of."

Cyn glanced up, waiting for him to interrupt, ask her to stay, something. But Jericho sat there, eyes never leaving her face, hands resting quietly on the tabletop, waiting.

"But I can't shut you out, Jericho. I just don't know how, and it terrifies me."

Finally, he reached across the table and took her restless hand in his. "Cynthia." *His voice is chocolate,* she thought, *pure, dark chocolate.* "I'm afraid, too." Dark fingers curved over hers, angry red welts still visible where they had been burnt by the fire, sheltering her without trying to hold on. "Look at me. Please." Brown eyes met black, both reflecting hurt and uncertainty. "Peace is not a town, my Cynthia." His soft voice cut through the chatter of the coffee shop. "Peace is that part of me that was missing before I found you. I'm not a man who needs or wants people to make me happy. All I've ever needed is the land and my horses." His callused hands tightened over hers before letting go abruptly, leaving her suddenly cold in Eric's overheated atmosphere.

Testing the limits of her courage, Cyn placed a pale hand on Jericho's cheek. "I don't want to hurt you, Jericho. I'd never want to do that. But I can't walk away from my degree, the scholarship, a lifetime of dreams."

"I would never ask you to, Cyn," he answered. "I just need you to know that I do care for you, more than I most likely should. Don't cut me out of your present because you are afraid for the future." His voice was pitched low to be private, but the intensity in it burned Cynthia with every word. "I'm here, Cynthia, and I'll always be here when you need me. Always."

Giving her hand a reassuring squeeze, Jericho stood up and wandered to the long counter at the back of the café, paid their tab, and with a final heated look at Cyn loped out the door into the mid-December snow.

Cyn's head dropped to where her crossed arms rested on the table, mind running in frantic circles trying to make sense of what Jericho had said. *What do I do with that? How could he make me a promise like that, knowing that I can't, maybe ever, make one back?*

Chapter 9

"Hurry up, Cyn, or we'll be late!" Bev's voice hustled Cyn out of the house early on a frigid Wednesday.

"What the hell, Mama?" Cyn growled. She needed her coffee, badly. "There aren't any clients until this afternoon. Why are you in such an ungodly rush today?"

"We have a nine o'clock appointment with my lawyer today and he's only in Peace for the morning. Get moving."

Grabbing the biggest to-go cup she could find, Cyn filled it with coffee, added extra sugar to replace the breakfast she wasn't going to get, and grouched her way out to the car. Shocked, she found that Mama wasn't just outside waiting but had already started the car and was sitting in the driver's seat. "You forgot that I know how to drive?" Bev joked. "I didn't drive when I was ill, but I'm a big girl, Cyn, I can do big girl stuff."

Skillfully manoeuvring around the snowdrifts at the entrance to the trailer park, Bev left Cyn alone to suck back her coffee and chew on the fact that Bev just didn't need her for everything anymore.

Pulling into the parking lot outside the town administration office, Bev turned to look at her daughter. "Cyn," she said with an odd twinkle in her dark eyes. "Today is going to be weird, and I know you won't like it. But good things are happening, little bird, very good things. Let's go face them!"

"Mr. Newcombe will be with you in a moment," the grey-haired receptionist for the Peace Administration Office said as she settled them in an office that smelled like old books and stale coffee. "He arrived from Billings earlier today and is just sorting through his files." The weak December sunshine was slipping through the vertical blinds and leaving unfortunate cell-bar patterns on the desk and wall.

"Good afternoon, ladies," Mr. Newcombe said, coming into the room from the main reception area. "Ms. Redman," he looked at Bev and nodded politely. "It's good to see you again. And you also, Cynthia."

Edward Newcombe settled himself behind the office desk and pulled a pad of lined paper toward himself.

Brushing his long fingers over his close-cut greying beard, he looked intently at Bev and asked, "For the record, Ms. Redman, do you understand the purpose of this meeting today?"

Bev nodded, leaving Cyn more confused than ever. *Mom didn't tell me about this,* Cyn muttered under her breath. *Why do we need to see Mr. Newcombe? Maybe it's something to do with what she calls The Problem Case.* Bev had taken the bus to Billings a couple of times, on her own, for appointments in the last few weeks. *I bet that it was Mr. Newcombe that she was seeing,* Cyn thought.

Adjusting his glasses, Mr. Newcombe smiled kindly. "Your mother and I have met several times in the last few weeks," he confirmed, his pleasant baritone at odds with the deliberately formal-looking room. "There are two separate issues that we need to discuss today. One involves you directly, Cynthia, and one does not, at least not specifically."

"Please," Cyn interrupted, "call me Cyn."

Mr. Newcombe nodded absentmindedly and went back to making notes on the paper. "Very well," he said. "Cyn. First, if I may, a bit of history."

Cyn rubbed idly at the frown lines between her eyes. *Couldn't they just get on with whatever the hell this was!*

"I know this is confusing," Bev said, smiling at Cyn sympathetically, "but it will make sense in the end, just hold on."

"Ms. Redman and I have known each other for more than 20 years," Mr. Newcombe announced.

Cyn blinked rapidly, eyes flashing back and forth between the smiling face of her mom and the angular one of the lawyer. She was sure that she had never met this aesthetic-looking man before. "Shortly after you were born, Miss. erm...Cyn," Mr. Newcombe continued, seeming not to notice Cyn's dismay, "Ms. Redman came to me to draft the articles of incorporation for her first practice in Billings. I have handled her corporate work ever since. Of course, we've spoken regularly this year, given the circumstances." Mr. Newcombe waved one hand at Bev, seeming to encompass everything about the frail figure across the desk.

"Mama?" Cyn's voice rose sharply. "The doctors said you were okay, they said that they got all the tumour. What the...?"

"Shush now." Bev's voice was soft but determined. "What the doctors said was true, and I am thankful. But just in case, I wanted to make sure my affairs were in order, and Edward has been helping me with that."

Cyn's eyebrow tried to bury itself in her hair. *Affairs? Did my mom just say affairs? She couldn't mean... No, she just couldn't, but she called him Edward.*

"I mean my *Will*, silly girl." Bev's eyes twinkled as she watched Cyn's mind race off, speculating wildly. "Edward drafted my Will just after you were born. I never thought that I would need to revise or review it, but now, I do."

Shaking her head, Cyn rubbed the frown lines between her eyes and tried to make sense of what she was hearing. "But why does changing your Will involve me?" she asked. "You can't honestly think I care about anything other than you being here, with me, alive!"

"Cyn, just listen, will you. I promise it will make sense at the end." Bev turned to Mr. Newcombe and nodded encouragingly. "I'm sorry, Edward, continue please."

"Ms. Redman"—he gestured at Bev—"had concerns about the wording of her Will. We have dealt with those issues in our previous meetings and she needs to sign it this morning."

Mr. Newcombe paused, for effect it seemed. Cyn felt like someone was driving a tank around inside her stomach. She had heard of a tense silence, but this was an intense one. It had weight and substance and seemed about to explode.

"Bev." Mr. Newcombe looked pointedly up at the clock on the wall. "Would you like me to leave you and Cyn for a little while? I know we have a time limit this morning, but this is, above all, a family matter."

Bev nodded. "Please, Edward. Just for a few minutes."

Grabbing his battered tan briefcase, Mr. Newcombe bustled out and quietly shut the door behind him.

"Mama," Cyn's words tumbled out like a waterfall, all the things she hadn't been able to say in front of the lawyer, now fighting each other to get out, "please, just tell me what's going on!"

Bev looked at her hands, twisting restlessly on her lap. "This is hard, little bird," she said. "A secret I've kept for so many years. When Edward first drafted my Will, I had no idea that I would...that *we* would ever come back to live in Peace."

Leaning forward, Cyn grabbed her mom's hands and held them still. "It doesn't matter," she said. "If it's this hard to tell me, then I don't need to know. Let's just get out of here and go for coffee."

"No, this is important, Cyn." Bev took a deep breath to calm herself and said, "It's about your father."

Cyn was beyond shocked. They had never talked about her father. As a teenager, she had pushed Bev over and over to tell her about her father and had been told that it was just one of those things. She had heard the unstated *don't ask* in her mom's voice and eventually had given up on finding out. "You don't want to tell me. You never have wanted to talk about it." Cyn shook her head, the dark braid flopping across her shoulder. "Why should it matter now?"

Bev took in a sharp breath and blurted out, "Your father was Brent Harrington."

"You're wrong, Mom. You have to be!" Cyn shuddered. The head of the Harrington Mafia and her mom? Not a chance!

"I'm not wrong, dear." Bev smiled reminiscently. "I was there. We dated in high school and planned to marry, but his dad didn't think a flathead Indian was good enough for his boy, so they sent Brent to college out east for a year and then"—Bev coughed embarrassedly—"convinced me that it was worth my while to get out of town before he returned. Especially when Brent's dad found out that I was pregnant."

I don't need to be a psychic to read between those lines, Cyn thought angrily, *I've heard what kind of convincing the Harringtons did when they wanted to get rid of someone.*

"I was a bit wild back then, Cyn," she said, swallowing thickly. "They said I would never be able to prove that you were Brent's, that they would use my past against me. There was no way I could have afforded a paternity test back then." Bev let out a heavy sigh. "Brent didn't know about you. I didn't know I was pregnant until after he left. But, it was obvious by the time he left that he didn't really love me, maybe he couldn't, being brought up the way he was, and I wasn't having the elder Harringtons anywhere near you. So, I took their money and went to Billings and got a job as the receptionist for Edward's Law Firm."

Cyn's world was rocking, and her hand had a white-knuckled grip on the edge of the big wooden desk. "You came back? How the hell could you come crawling back to Peace after all that!"

Bev's eyes hardened. "I do not—did not ever—crawl!" Her voice was as cold as the snow that blew against the office window. "I came back because I was finally in a position to help the people that the Harringtons were hurting." One frail hand touched Cyn's face gently. "Don't cry, little bird. It will be well, you'll see." Cyn was still shaking, her emotions racing like a prairie blizzard. She hadn't even realized that she was crying. "Brent's gone now, maybe at peace finally, and his death ends the story. Except for this."

Cyn's eyes felt like all the gravel on the highway was stuck in them. *What more could there be?*

"As the only living Harrington by blood," Bev said, her face serious, her voice calm and determined, "you have a claim on Brent's estate, and I mean you to take it."

Cyn stood up, pacing back and forth across the worn carpet like a caged wolf. "You think I'd take anything from them, after all the things that family has done to Peace, the way they treated you? Mama, *no!*"

"Listen, Cyn. Calm down and listen." Bev spoke slowly, trying to get through the whirlwind in Cyn's mind, "This is your college money, it's a decent house, it's so many things that we have always wanted, and it brings to you all the benefits the older Harringtons didn't want you to have."

Cyn sat with a thump, not realizing that she was in Mr. Newcombe's chair.

"It's blood money," she said, shaking her head.

"Yes, it is," Bev replied unexpectedly. "But in the very best way. And strangely enough, it is what Brent, what your father, wanted."

"He's not my father," Cyn answered reflexively, then caught herself on the last part of Bev's statement. "How do you know what Brent wanted?"

"Edward," Bev answered succinctly. "Brent's Will was probated after his death and he left his entire estate to '*whoever is proven to be my closest blood relation.*' That's you. His name is on your birth certificate and his blood will show on a DNA test." Cyn was pacing again, shoving her hands into her hair and completely undoing the dishevelled braid hanging over her shoulder. "Just give yourself some time, Cyn."

Mama sounds far too reasonable, Cyn thought. *How can I just "give it time" when everything I know about who I am has been shattered?*

Cyn jumped as Mr. Newcombe opened the office door and walked in carrying a tray of coffees from Generic Eric's. "Black, two sugars for you, Bev." He handed her a tall to-go cup and turned to put the tray down in front of Cyn. "I wasn't sure what you wanted, so sugar and creamer are on the tray." Mr. Newcombe sat down and reorganized the papers on the desk, adjusted his glasses, and said, "Are we ready to move on to item number two? The second item is a matter of professional misconduct and is completely unrelated to the first." Mr. Newcombe's voice dropped into a deeper pitch and his language became precise and devoid of emotion. "Namely, can Ms. Redman"— he gestured at Bev, obviously being specific—"be held professionally liable if she reveals criminal actions, committed by her client, to the police."

Cyn was paying attention again. She remembered how troubled her mom had been on their trip to Helena and all the reading and research that Bev had done since. It hadn't occurred to Cyn to wonder where all those law texts came from. Now she knew. Mr. Newcombe had sent them. She glanced sideways at her mom and nodded toward the door. Bev shook her head and glanced down at the table, a definite *no, stay.*

"Remember when we went to Helena?" she asked.

"Of course," Cyn replied. "We talked a bit about this at the campground."

"I told you that I wouldn't leave you in the dark," Bev continued, ignoring Cyn's interruption. "Now it's time to fill you in. This relates to a crime committed, or believed to be committed, by one of my clients."

"Believed to be committed?" Cyn's voice mimicked Bev's professional monotone. "What the hell are you talking about, Mama?"

Bev's nose wrinkled comically.

"Not funny, Mama."

"No," Bev responded. "I suppose not, but in a way, it is very ironic."

Mr. Newcombe reached into his briefcase and handed them each a sheaf of photocopied papers. "Bev," he said, his voice formal, but not cold. "You have a decision to make. If you go to the police with what your patient has told you, you may be sending your patient to jail."

"But," Cyn interrupted forcefully, "if this person has committed a crime..."

Mr. Newcombe shook his head firmly. "That isn't enough in this case, Cynthia." Cyn glared at the lawyer but was cut off before she could remind him to call her Cyn. No one used Cynthia, ever...well, almost no one. "Because there is a psychological professional involved, a different level of responsibility has to be considered." Picking up one of the papers on the desk, he pointed to a paragraph circled in neon blue. "This is the section I was talking about, Bev," he said. "The Montana Code for Mental Health Professionals sets out three specific requirements before you can break client confidentiality and I don't think your client meets all three of those. From what you've told me, Bev, your client believes they committed a crime?"

Bev nodded. She looked amazingly calm and serene, in stark contrast to the frenetic energy that was swirling around Cyn.

"But what can Mama do?" Cyn interjected trying to get something solid to hold on to in a world that had been turned upside down twice in the space of an hour.

Bev grabbed Cyn's hand and tugged her back into a seat. "Calm down, Cyn," she said. "This is what Edward does. Listen and learn."

Cyn grumbled under her breath, trying to hang on, to rein in her impatience.

"May I continue?" Mr. Newcombe inquired. "Our time is unfortunately limited today."

"Of course, Edward." Bev smiled warmly at the solemn lawyer. "Aren't you glad you don't have such fractious womenfolk to deal with all the time!"

Edward smiled, years dropping from his expression. "You know me very well, even now. Much too demanding." Tapping on the pad of paper, he continued. "So, we have a client who believes they committed a crime. Point One. But, two and three are where it gets more difficult. 'Is this person mentally capable of understanding what they did, or think they did?' And Three, 'Did they commit the crime, or are they merely convinced that they did?' I can't answer those questions for you, Bev." Edward reached across the desk and took Bev's hand. "All I can tell you for sure is that if you have any doubt that your client meets all three of these points, you cannot go to the police without losing your professional qualifications and possibly opening yourself for both criminal and civil liability."

Bev and Edward talked for a few more minutes, then the grey-haired lawyer ushered them out with a final encouragement. "Call if you need me," he said. "I'm only an hour away."

Chapter 10

The ride home was silent, weighty, and uncomfortable. Cyn drove this time, manoeuvring the old Prius around the snowdrifts and through the ruts without thinking. Ninety percent of her mind was desperately trying to bring some sense into her upside-down world.

Finally, seated at the chipped green table, she stared at her mom, trying to find something coherent to say.

"Are you okay, little bird?" Bev's voice was quiet, and her face looked pale and tired.

"I'm not sure," Cyn replied honestly. "I don't think I know who I am anymore."

"Fiddlesticks," Bev interjected. "You are the same amazing person I raised; smart, loving, and just a bit of a control freak. Change happens, Cyn." Bev reached out and gripped Cyn's hands as they lay clutched on the tabletop. "This will be a good change, you'll see."

"Does this mean you can keep the clinic open, Mama?" Cyn asked. She knew that Bev had poured every penny they had into that storefront clinic and that it had broken her heart to realize that they would have to let the lease drop.

"I don't know, Cyn," Bev answered. "The estate will be yours, not mine."

"It's not a question, then," Cyn said, shoulders square, arms folded across her chest. "You call the realtors and have them cancel the sublease."

"Estates don't finish up that quickly, Cyn," Bev explained. "Edward is a good lawyer and has worked on probates for years, but it will be well into spring before you can expect to see anything coming your way." A thoughtful look danced over her expressive features as she continued, "Although, I suppose we can take the proof of your inheritance, and your paperwork from the University to the bank and get a loan against the probate. I'm sure Edward would write up whatever kind of letter they need."

Cyn's smile was electric. "We can win, Mama," she said. "Finally, after it all settles, we win!" Pulling a notepad from the counter and grabbing a pen from the top of the avocado-coloured 1970s fridge, Cyn started her wish list. "There are so many things we need. I can't even start planning. We need to keep the clinic open and find a new receptionist. I need to confirm my course list for the spring semester at M.S.U."

"Slow down, little bird." Bev laughed joyfully. "It's good to see you planning your future, but we have some things to get through before this can happen."

Chapter 11

The normal downhill rush from Thanksgiving to Christmas had been muted a bit this year to accommodate Bev's energy level.

Still, Cyn thought, gazing into the artificial tree set up in the clinic's reception area, *things couldn't be more perfect, at least on the outside.* Cyn had always been fascinated by Christmas trees. She would spend hours looking between the branches and lights, into the empty spaces that opened into a magical world full of light and illusion.

I've got more to be thankful for this year than ever before, she thought. *Mama is getting better, Jericho is upset that I'm leaving, even though he is happy that I can go to school, but he is willing to see if we can handle a long-distance relationship until I finish my degree, and David Falton is spending Christmas in the Billings jail waiting for a trial date.*

December 20th was the last office day before the clinic closed for Christmas—but not forever. A firm letter to the realtors from Mr. Newcombe and a loan from the Great Plains Credit Union had guaranteed that the clinic would be open, at least part time, while Bev recovered. Clients were being rebooked into January and the hunt was on for a receptionist to take Cyn's place when she left for Bozeman for the January semester.

At ten o'clock, the front door jangled, shaking the bright-white mistletoe that Bev had hung on the doorknob.

"Merry Christmas," Cyn greeted the elderly client with a polite nod. "Are you all packed up and ready to go?"

Mrs. Webster was leaving for Deer Lodge on the weekend to spend Christmas with her grandchildren and, if things worked out, she wouldn't be coming back.

"May I take your coat? Cyn said as she ushered Mrs. Webster into the treatment room its muted lighting and ambient music creating a warm, safe atmosphere. "Dr. Redman will be with you in a minute."

Glancing down the hallway, Cyn frowned, noticing that the door to her mom's office was closed. Tapping her fingers impatiently on the reception desk, Cyn waited a minute or two for Bev to come out. When nothing happened, she picked up the telephone and called the back office herself. "Mama, Mrs. Webster is in the treatment room," she said a bit brusquely. It wasn't good practice to make clients sit and wait.

"I'm coming, Cyn." Bev's voice sounded unusually defensive. "I was on the phone with Edward."

Again? Cyn thought. Cyn knew that her mom had called Mr. Newcombe three times the day before, and now she was calling him again? *I wonder what they are going to spring on me next,* she thought, lips pursing. *I don't think I can take one more surprise revelation.*

Walking carefully down the long hallway from her office, Bev Redman looked almost overbalanced by the weight of the books and files she was carrying. Dropping a folded sheet of paper on the reception desk, she nodded in Cyn's general direction, looked intentionally at the page, and opened the door to the treatment room. "Good morning, Betty," she said quietly to the patient Mrs. Webster. "I'm sorry I was delayed."

Cyn frowned at the folded paper on her desk. Her mother had scrawled her name on the outside along with explicit instructions to open the paper after her session with Betty Webster began. Opening the single page, she read:

Cyn,

> *This appointment is going to be difficult. Please, don't leave the desk. I might need you to make an emergency call. Don't worry.*

~Mom

For the next hour Cyn paced back and forth across the small reception area, hands clenching and unclenching, shoulders locked up tight, eyes flashing to the door of the treatment room every two seconds. *I'm wearing a bald spot in the carpet,* she thought. *Don't worry? What the hell else did Mama think I would be doing, after getting a note like that?*

When the door to the treatment room slammed open and Mrs. Webster hobbled out, shaking her cane at where Bev stood in the doorway, Cyn jumped so violently that the paper in her hands was torn in two.

"I don't know what I expected," Mrs. Webster protested. "If anyone in this rotten town understood that Brent Harrington had to die, I would think it was you!"

"Betty, calm down," Bev spoke calmly, reasonably, in the voice Cyn grew up calling her Counsellor Redman Voice. "Come back in and let's finish up."

"I will not be talked to like a child, Beverly Redman." Mrs. Webster's face was flushed with anger and her normally pleasant voice had sharpened into a brittle falsetto. "I've known you since *you* were a child. Don't you 'calm down' to me!"

"Betty..." Bev couldn't get another word out as Mrs. Webster grabbed her coat and swung around, once again shaking the paisley cane in her face.

"Brent raped my daughter, Bev! Left her pregnant and alone. She killed herself. But he got away with it. And why? Because he was a goddamned Harrington! Do you think that going to jail would change him? That he would learn anything? No! Someone had to make him pay for Kathleen's life. He had to pay, and I took care of it. It was perfect."

"Betty." Cyn glanced at the phone and at her mom. *Do I need to call the police?* Bev shook her head, an almost imperceptible no. "I don't think we want to talk about this in front of people."

"In front of Brent's bastard, you mean?" The old lady glared at Cyn, eyes glazed with an almost irrational hatred, as though Cyn was responsible for the actions of a father she had never known. "You don't think that the whole town knows? We always suspected it, now it's proven, the Harringtons paid you off to leave town with his little embarrassment…"

Cyn didn't know where to look as Mrs. Webster ranted *How do I deal with this,* she thought, worrying at her bottom lip. *Is there any way that I can still be me, knowing that all the pain Brent Harrington caused is a part of who I am.*

Mrs. Webster stopped pacing back and forth long enough to glare at Bev. "It took me three months in Deer Lodge to get the volunteer position cooking at the prison," she said resentfully.

Betty's mind is wandering, Cyn thought fighting against the need to defend her mom, defend herself from this undeserved tirade. *She doesn't even know that there are people here. Maybe she's just trying to convince herself that her revenge worked?*

"I put the blood-thinners in his food," Betty continued, pacing along the same rut in the old Navajo carpet that Cyn had a few minutes earlier. "I knew that he would start throwing his weight around sooner or later and that someone would do the hard part for me. All it took was a bad punch and he bled to death. Poor Prisoner 8477. All dead."

Bev glanced at Cyn and mouthed the word *Prius*. It was their code word for making an emergency call.

Mrs. Webster was standing in the middle of the reception area, babbling incoherently, spittle running from one side of her mouth, cane hanging limply from her unguided hand. Although the elderly lady was obviously no physical threat to them, she was certainly at the point where she could hurt herself if she tried to leave.

Reaching under the desk, Cyn pressed the emergency call button twice, knowing that someone in the Sheriff's office, hopefully Dray, would get the message and that the two lights would let them know it was a medical problem.

Dray burst into the clinic a few minutes later, just as Mrs. Webster collapsed to lie like a broken doll on the clinic floor. "What the hell?" Dray Palmer shoved a distracted hand through his hair. "The medics are on the way, but there wasn't anyone in town, so it will be a few minutes. What are we dealing with?"

"She's overwrought," Bev explained. "We were talking about her daughter's death, it was just too much for her." Cyn glanced sharply at her mom. That was a seriously watered-down version of affairs. *Is Mama trying to lie to the police?*

Bev shook her head at Cyn and mouthed *Let it go.*

"She has a heart condition," Cyn reminded Dray as he fussed over the older woman. "I don't know if she has medication. Maybe check her purse." Rummaging through Mrs. Webster's purse produced a small bottle of nitroglycerin spray. After reading the instructions, Dray decided that it wouldn't be safe to guess about her condition. All they could do was try and make Mrs. Webster comfortable until the medic arrived.

Cyn was almost vibrating with the tension by the time they had stabilized Mrs. Webster and transported her to the hospital. *Would mama tell Dray what happened—why Betty collapsed?* But she didn't. Bev calmly thanked Dray and the medics and locked the door behind them. Only after they had gone did she slump into one of the waiting room chairs, breathing deeply.

"It's over," Bev said.

"What do you mean, Mama?" Cyn was so confused. *Nothing was over,* she thought. "As soon as Mrs. Webster wakes up she'll talk and the whole ugly mess will start again." Stomach churning, head pounding from the tension, Cyn stalked back and forth across the small reception area. "All the things she said, the accusations, is this what living in Peace is going to be like now? It was bad enough when people didn't know."

"I don't think we need to worry about the town, or about Betty," Bev continued. "This is nothing but a thunderstorm in a town like Peace, everyone will soon move on to the next piece of gossip." Catching Cyn's arm as she stalked past, Bev pulled her down into one of the reception chairs. "Sit down, child.

Do you remember the three points that Edward said we needed to prove before I could report Betty to the police? She had to admit to the crime, she had to be mentally capable of understanding the crime, and she had to have actually committed the crime."

"Yes?" Cyn's eyebrows scrunched up in puzzlement, forming a ridge that was almost painful.

"Do you believe that anyone would believe that Betty Webster, as she was today, is capable of planning and committing a murder?"

"But—" Cyn's question was waved away.

"Besides," Bev gloated. "I got the proof today—she didn't kill him, even if she thought she had."

That's it! Cyn fumed. *Either mom is going to explain this, or I'm going to end up a patient in my own psych. hospital.*

"I asked Edward to look into the autopsy report." Bev smiled, that smug adult smile that had made Cyn feel so rebellious as a teenager. "There were no blood-thinners found in Brent's toxicology screen. They do a full drug panel for any violent death in a State Prison." Bev's head dropped onto the back of the lounge chair. "So, she didn't do it, even if she thinks she did. And if it helps her to believe Kathleen has been avenged, who am I to take that from her? It's over."

Cyn faked a smile, not quite believing that the world would ever be normal. *These changes were too much,* she thought, *it would never be over.*

Still, she thought to herself. *It's almost Christmas, Mama is getting better, the cloud over the practice has blown away, and I am going to get my degree and hopefully Jericho will wait for me. So really, I have to admit I'm blessed.*

Chapter 12

The Christmas season drifted past buried by a flurry of tinsel and bright with a promise of new adventures. *The New Year has finally begun* Cyn thought *and tomorrow so will my new life in Bozeman.* Taking a deep breath for courage, she stepped into the light and music filling Toppin's Bar. *But first comes tonight, and one last date with Jericho.*

"So, you showed up." Jericho's soft voice hit Cyn's heart like a shot of Jack Daniels. "I was starting to wonder."

I should be stronger, Cyn thought. But as Jericho pulled her in to lean against the blue denim of his shirt, laundered soft as a spring morning, she felt safe. At peace with herself and the world for the first time since Bev got sick and David Falton went to jail.

"I shouldn't have come," Cyn said. "I don't want to be here, but I don't want to be anywhere else—it makes no sense." She tried to step back, but Jericho's arms were strong and warm. Not holding tight, as if he knew she'd bolt if he did, just being there. Cyn gave up. Her head dropped into the niche just beneath his shoulder. She fit so perfectly against him.

"I'm not going to pressure you, Cyn. You know that's not me." Jericho looked down with so much compassion that Cyn felt her heart break.

How could I walk away from him? her heart cried. *How could I even think of it! How could someone so gentle, so quiet, be in love with someone like me? The last by-blow of the Harrington curse.*

"You're thinking too much." The half smile on Jericho's face took the sting out of the words. His hand moved slowly from where it rested on Cyn's waist and slid up to the nape of her neck. "Don't worry about it, my Cynthia. I'm not leaving you."

Cyn's eyes burned. "Damn you, Jericho Matthews!" she cussed him out under her breath. "Stop being so damned perfect. How can I leave you when you make it so easy to stay?"

You need to go, little bird. Bev's voice in the back of Cyn's head seemed to wrap around the sappy country music the old jukebox was playing. *This is your dream, you've worked for it, you've made it happen. If you are his dream he will wait for you to return.*

It was the memory of her mother's words that finally broke Cyn's control. She cried, real tears, not the Hollywood perfect-goodbye kind of tears that she'd planned. *Oh great*, she snuffled to herself. *My nose is red and my eyes look like I lost a prizefight.*

Grabbing a napkin from the nearest scuffed wooden table, Jericho wiped Cyn's face, gently crooning nonsense words into her hair. Turning her face toward him, his lips touched Cyn's gently. Not a real kiss, just a promise. "I'll be here, little bird," he said, dark eyes blazing. "I will always be here for you."

"How did you know!" Cyn hiccupped. Words were a bit of a problem when her nose was snotty and tears were clogging her throat. "How did you know that name? No one knows it!"

His diffident smile rested on her like a benediction. "I talked to your momma at Christmas. Asked her permission to court you if you would have me. She told me that her little bird would need to fly, but if I held on loosely, that you would always come home when your wings grew tired. I didn't know it was a name," he said, "I thought your mom was just describing you."

"It's my traditional name," Cyn said. "Only family are supposed to know it." Brow furrowed, Cyn continued, "If mama told you, then she considered you family. Trusted you."

"You are my family, Cyn." He turned her eyes up to meet his. One firm hand stroked up and down her back like he was gentling one of the horses he loved so much. "You are my future, my campfire, my warm place in the night." His words burned into Cyn's heart. "I know you have to go, love. You need to fly. But I will be here waiting for you to bring my heart home."

The night could have lasted forever. Cyn and Jericho danced to every hokey song the old jukebox held and talked in whispers. Until finally, last round was called, and they stepped into the cold December air. Walking in silence from Toppins Bar to the motel where Jericho was staying for the night, she wondered what would happen now and where that decision would take them.

"Jericho?" Cyn's voice was shaky. This wasn't her first dance, but she felt like the most unbroken filly in the pasture. Jericho's arm was strong around her shoulders. He wasn't trying to steer her progress, just keeping in touch with where she wanted to go. "Jericho?"

Cyn's voice was a bit stronger this time. *Does he really need me to say it?* She thought, panicking, *Does he not want me?*

"Cyn." His voice sounded strained, deeper than she'd ever heard him speak. His hands gripped Cyn's shoulders tightly, not hurting, but not backing off, and this time when they kissed it made a beginning, crossed that line that she'd never dared breach before. "I love you and I need you like a drunkard needs whiskey. But we can't do this." His forehead rested against hers and she could feel his heart racing.

"Why? Why can't we?" Somewhere in Cyn's mind a voice was screaming at her. She was leaving tomorrow. But all Cyn could see were those dark eyes burning into her with such need written in them.

"One sip of water will not save a dying man," he said, and Cyn could feel him taking shuddering breaths, grasping desperately for control. "One night with you, knowing you are leaving tomorrow, would drive me mad. I couldn't let you go, and you need to go. You need me to let you go." Warm hands framed her face as Jericho's lips descended on hers. "My Cynthia," he said thickly, "come home to me." Then slipping his beloved Stetson onto her head, he turned away releasing her to her dreams.

Chapter 13

Piling her stuff into the back of the rented van didn't seem to take as long as she wanted it to. Cyn was glad that Jericho hadn't come to see her off. They had danced for hours last night, just swaying to the melodies of those old cowboys her mom had loved so much. She could still feel the warmth of Jericho's arms and the tickle of his breath against her ear. He had whispered a promise, and she knew he would keep it. George Jones had told her so.

"If I can't be your first love, I'll wait and be your last, I'll be here in your future, to help you forget your past, and you'll know that I've loved you with a love that's sincere, 'cause I'll wait till you're done living through your tender years."

Finally, the van was loaded and gassed up, everything done and ready. The lump in her throat almost choked her as Cyn drove past the no-name hotel and saw Jericho leaning against his still dented pickup truck, wiry black hair shining, one leg casually propped on the running board, hand shielding his eyes from the early morning sun, or maybe hiding what might have been tears.

The highway opened up before her, leaving nothing visible of home except the "Welcome to Peace" sign at the town limits.

I'll be back, she promised herself. Promised him. *As soon as I finish my degree, I'll be home. But for now...Peace out.*

Epilogue

6:45 a.m.

Cyn groaned, rolled over, and swatted at the screeching beast on her nightstand. After a few minutes of flailing, she managed to hit the snooze button and hunkered down for that priceless five minutes before the madness started again.

One heavy sigh, a rustle of bedding, and she gave up. Stretching in the cold of her college dorm room, Cyn quickly started up the coffee pot and dove for the shower. A few minutes later, warm and dressed, she settled at her desk. Half an hour before she had to leave for class, time to get organized for the day. Her desk was a typical muddle of papers and coffee cup rings. In the middle, jammed between her copies of "Proust Was a Neuroscientist" and "Mapping the Mind" was a threadbare black Stetson and small flip calendar. Running a gentle hand over the hat and picking up the calendar, Cyn grabbed her red pen, she marked a bold X across the date. Three more weeks and she would be going home. Home to Peace.

To my readers

Thank you for sharing Cyn and Jericho's story with me.

If you enjoyed this book, please let others know. Most people will trust the word of a friend over any amount of advertising.

Also, leave a review! Reviews are hugs to an author, they cost you nothing, but we aren't be happy without them!

I'd love to hear from you, so please check me out on social media.

... Sandra

Social Media Links:

Facebook:
www.facebook.com/SandraHurst.Author
Twitter: *www.twitter.com/SandraHurst*
Blog: *www.delusionsofliteracy.com*
Email: *mailto:sandrahurstauthor@gmail.com*

About the Author

A mythmaker at heart, Sandra Hurst has been writing poetry, fantasy, romance, and science fiction since her school days in England. Hurst moved to Canada in 1980 and was deeply influenced by the wild lands and the indigenous cultures that surrounded her.

Her first novel, Y'keta, is long-listed for the prestigious Aurora Award, for best Canadian fantasy novel (Young Adult) and the American-based RONE award for best New Adult novel of 2017.

She now lives in Calgary, Alberta with her husband and son, both of whom she loves dearly, and has put up for sale on e-bay when their behaviour demanded it.

Y'keta

A young exile finds a place to belong, only to find his new home threatened by secrets from his past. If Y'keta reveals what he knows to the villagers, it will tear their history and traditions apart, but sharing his secrets may be their only hope for survival.

Y'keta is an epic fantasy set in an ancient world, where legends walk, and the Sky Road offers a way to the stars.

A coming of age story, with colours reminiscent of the early works of Guy Gavriel Kay or Piers Anthony.

https://www.amazon.com/dp/B01N9V4M8C

The Peace Series

Welcome to our small Montana town. Here, love runs free and often appears unexpectedly. Settle in. Look around. You may just discover your happily ever after. Follow this amazing crossover series, as authors from every different genre and background bring the people of Peace to life!

A. H. Stagg - 'Songs of Peace'
Krysi Foster - 'Love in Peace'
L. C. Fenton - 'What Peace Remains'
S. H. Pratt - 'Reclaiming Peace'
Cassie May - 'Seeking Peace'
Cassie May - 'A Haven in Peace'
Lisa Ann - 'Peace and Harmony'
Jennifer Fisch-Ferguson - 'The Philosophy of Peace'
Gabriela Lizette - 'Beautiful MasterPeace'
Punam Farmah - 'Retreating to Peace'
Jeanetta S. Tarver - Peace and Comfort
Caroline Andrus - Peace in Flames
Jenn Bradock - Accepting Peace
Tee Smith - A Dusty Road to Peace
S. Jackson Rivera - Peace in the Storm
Caroline Andrus – Summer of Peace
Rachel Waters – Peace of Me